ADRIFT
on the
NILE

*The following titles by Naguib Mahfouz
are also published by Doubleday and Anchor Books:*

THE THIEF AND THE DOGS

THE BEGINNING AND THE END

WEDDING SONG

THE BEGGAR

RESPECTED SIR

AUTUMN QUAIL

THE TIME AND THE PLACE and Other Stories

THE SEARCH

MIDAQ ALLEY

THE JOURNEY OF IBN FATTOUMA

The Cairo Trilogy:

PALACE WALK

PALACE OF DESIRE

SUGAR STREET

Naguib Mahfouz

ADRIFT on the NILE

Translated by
Frances Liardet

DOUBLEDAY

New York London Toronto Sydney Auckland

PUBLISHED BY DOUBLEDAY
a division of Bantam Doubleday Dell Publishing Group, Inc.
666 Fifth Avenue, New York, NY 10103

DOUBLEDAY and the portrayal of an anchor with
a dolphin are trademarks of Doubleday,
a division of Bantam Doubleday Dell
Publishing Group, Inc.

Adrift on the Nile was first published in Arabic in 1966,
under the title *Tharthara Fawq al Nil.*

This translation is published by arrangement with The American
University in Cairo Press.

*I would like to thank Dr. Sabry Hafiz of SOAS London for his enthusiastic advice on the final
draft of this translation. Any remaining faults are mine alone.—Frances Liardet*

Library of Congress Cataloging-in-Publication Data

Maḥfūẓ, Najīb, 1912-
    [Thartharah fawqa al-Nīl. English]
    Adrift on the Nile / Naguib Mahfouz : translated by Frances Liardet.
        p.   cm.
    Translation of: Thartharah fawqa al-Nīl.
    I. Title.
    PJ7846.A46T513   1993
    892'.736—dc20   92-20977
                                                 CIP

ISBN 0-385-42322-5
Copyright © 1966 by Naguib Mahfouz
English translation copyright © 1993 by Frances Liardet
ALL RIGHTS RESERVED
PRINTED IN THE UNITED STATES OF AMERICA
FEBRUARY 1993
FIRST EDITION

ADRIFT
on the
NILE

1 ❧

April. Month of dust and lies. The long, high-ceilinged office a gloomy storeroom for cigarette smoke. On the shelves the files enjoy an easeful death. How diverting they must find the civil servant at work, carrying out, with utterly serious mien, utterly trivial tasks. Recording the arrival of registered post. Filing. Incoming mail. Outgoing mail. Ants, cockroaches, and spiders, and the smell of dust stealing in through the closed windows.

"Have you finished that report?" the Head of Department asked.

Anis Zaki replied indolently. "Yes," he said. "I've sent it to the Director General."

The Head gave him a piercing look that glinted glassily, like a beam of light, through his thick spectacles. Had he caught Anis grinning like an imbecile at nothing? But people were used to putting up with such nonsense in April, month of dust and lies.

The Head of Department began to be overtaken by an odd, involuntary movement. It spread through all the parts of his body that could be seen above the desk—slow and undulating, but visibly progressing. Gradually, he began to swell up. The swelling spread from his chest to his neck, to his face, and then over his entire head. Anis stared fixedly at his boss as the swelling obliterated the features and contours of his face and finally turned the man into a great globe of flesh. It appeared that he had grown lighter in some astonishing way, for the globe proceeded to rise, slowly at first, and then gradually more swiftly, until it flew up like a gas balloon and stuck, bobbing, to the ceiling . . .

"Why are you looking at the ceiling, Mr. Zaki?" the Head of Department asked.

Caught again. Eyes stared at him in pitying mockery. Heads were shaken regretfully in ostentatious sympathy for the boss. Let the stars bear witness to that! Even the midges and the frogs have better manners. The asp itself did the Queen of Egypt a great favor. But you, my colleagues? There is no good in you; my only comfort lies in the words of that dear friend who said: "Come and live on the houseboat. You won't have to pay a millieme. Just get everything ready for us."

With sudden resolution he began to deal with a pile of letters. Dear Sir: With reference to your letter reference number 1911, dated February 2, 1964, and to the communication pertaining, reference number 2008, dated March 28, 1964: I have the honor of informing you . . . Filtering in along with the smell of dust, a song from a radio in the street: "Mama, the moon is at the door." He paused, pen in hand, and muttered: "Wonderful!"

"Lucky you, with no worries," said a colleague on his right.

Damn the lot of you. Timeservers every one. Waiting for a dream that will never come true, you turn your silly tricks. I am the only miracle here, speeding—without a rocket—into outer space . . .

The office boy came in. Anis felt his stomach rumble, and asked for one coffee, no sugar.

"You'll find it on your desk," the office boy replied, "when you come back from seeing the Director General." And so Anis, tall and big—heavy-boned, though, not fat—left the room.

Once in the Director General's office, he stood meekly in front of the desk. The Director's bald head remained bowed over the papers he was perusing, looking to Anis like an upturned boat . . . With his last scrap of willpower Anis drove away such distracting thoughts. Distraction at this point would have the most dire consequences.

The man lifted his lined, angular face to fix Anis with a bristling glare. What error could have crept into the report that he had taken such pains to compile?

"I asked you to write a detailed report on the movement of incoming correspondence for last month," the Director said.

"Yes, sir, and I've presented it to you, sir."

"Is this it?"

Anis glanced at the report. On the cover he read, in his own handwriting: *Report on Incoming Correspondence for the month of March—for the attention of the Director General of the Archives Department.*

"That's it, sir."

"Look at it and read it."

He saw one line, clearly written, followed by a blank

space. Dumbfounded, he turned over the remaining pages. Then he gaped like an imbecile at the Director General.

"Read it!" the man said angrily.

"Sir—I wrote it out word for word ..."

"Would you care to tell me how it has vanished?"

"Really, it's a complete mystery to me! ..."

"But you *can* see before you the marks made by the pen nib?"

"Marks made by the pen nib ... ?"

"Give me this magic pen of yours!" the Director said, and, brusquely taking the pen from Anis, he began to score lines on the cover of the report. None of the lines came out on the paper. "There isn't a single drop of ink in it!" said the Director.

Consternation spread over Anis' broad face.

"You began writing this line here, and then the ink ran out," the Director continued caustically. "But you carried on!"

Anis said nothing.

"You failed to notice that the pen was not writing!"

Anis made a perplexed gesture.

"Can you tell me, Mr. Zaki, how this could have happened?"

How indeed. How did life first creep into the mosses in the cracks of the rocks, in the ocean depths?

"You're not blind, as far as I'm aware, Mr. Zaki."

Anis hung his head.

"I shall answer for you. You did not see what was on the page, because you were ... drugged!"

"Sir!"

"It's the truth. And a truth which is known, further-more, to everyone right down to the office boys and porters. I am not a preacher. Nor am I responsible for your well-being. You may do with yourself as you please. But I have the right to demand that you refrain from doping yourself during working hours."

"Sir!"

"Enough sir-ing and demurring. Be so good as to comply with my humble request and leave your habit at home."

Anis protested. "As God is my witness—I am ill!"

"The eternal invalid, that is what you are."

"Don't believe what . . ."

"I only have to look into your eyes!"

"It's illness—nothing else!"

"All I can see is that your eyes are red, cloudy, heavy . . ."

"Don't listen to talk! . . ."

". . . and they look inward, instead of outward like the rest of God's creatures!"

The Director's hands, covered with bushy white hairs, made a threatening gesture. Sharply, he said: "There are limits to my patience. But there is no end to a slippery slope. Do not tumble down it. You are in your forties, which should be a time of maturity. So stop this tom-foolery."

Anis took two steps backward, preparing to leave.

"I shall only cut two days' pay from your salary," the man added. "But beware of any repetition of this episode."

As he moved toward the door, Anis heard the Director

General say contemptuously: "When will you learn the difference between a government department and a smoking den?"

On his return to the department, heads were raised and turned inquisitively in his direction. Ignoring them, he sat down and gazed at his cup of coffee. He became aware of a colleague leaning over to him, no doubt to ask him all about it. "Mind your own business," he muttered angrily.

He took an inkwell out of the drawer and began to fill his pen. He would have to rewrite the report. "Movement of Incoming Correspondence." It was not a movement at all, really. It was a revolution around a fixed axis, round and round, distracted by its own futility. Round and round it went, and the only thing that came of it was an endless revolution. And in the whirling giddiness everything of value disappeared: medicine and science and law, family forgotten back home in the village, a wife and small daughter lying under the earth. Words once blazing with zeal now buried under a mountain of ice . . .

Not a man was left on the road. The doors and windows were closed. And the dust flew up under the horses' hooves, and the Mameluke soldiery let loose yells of joy on the road to the hunt; any man abroad in the quarters of Margush or Gamaliya was made a target for their skill, and the victims' cries were drowned by the yells of mad joy, and the bereaved mother screamed: "Mercy, O kings!" and the hunter bore down on her on that day of sport; and the coffee grew cold and the taste of it changed, and the Mameluke still roared, grinning from ear to ear, and a headache came and the vision fled, and still the Mameluke laughed. And they hurled down curses and made the dust fly, reveling in splendor, reveling in torture . . .

A cheerful animation spread through the gloomy room. It was time to go home.

2

The houseboat lay still on the leaden waters of the Nile, as familiar to him as a face. To the right there was an empty space, once occupied by another houseboat before the current swept it away, and to the left, on a wide bank of the shore, a simple mosque surrounded by a mud-brick wall and spread with shabby matting. Anis approached the houseboat, passing through a white wooden gate in a hedge of violet and jasmine.

Amm Abduh, the night watchman, rose to greet him, his gigantic frame topping the slats and palm branches that composed the roof of his mud-brick hut. Anis made for the gangway of the houseboat, walking down a tiled path that was flanked on each side by a grassy space. To the right of the path, in the middle of the grass, there was a watercress bed, while far over to the left, a wilderness of hyacinth bean lay like a backdrop behind a towering guava tree. The sun's rays beat down, fierce and insistent, through an arbor of eucalyptus branches that spread from the roadside trees to shade the small garden.

He changed his clothes and went to sit, dressed in his long white tunic, in the doorway of the balcony overlooking the Nile. He welcomed the gentle breeze, letting it caress him tenderly, letting his eyes wander over the expanse of water, which could have been still and motionless, not a ripple, not a sparkle could he see. But it carried the voices clearly from the houseboats moored in a long line on the opposite bank, beneath the evergreens and acacia trees. He sighed, loud enough for Amm Abduh—who was setting the small table next to the right-hand wall, a couple of meters from the refrigerator—to ask him: "All's well, I hope?"

"A disgusting, rotten atmosphere today," Anis muttered, turning toward him. "Drove away my good mood."

"But you always come back in the end to the good atmosphere here."

The old man never ceased to excite his admiration. He was like something great and ancient, rooted in time. Vitality leaped from his deeply lined eyes. Perhaps those deep furrows were what awed him; or perhaps it was the clump of thick white hair that sprang like date blossoms from the neck of his robe. And the robe itself, coarse calico, hanging like a drape over a statue, hanging straight down unhindered. No flesh, really, just skin and bone. But what bones! He was built like a giant, and his head grazed the ceiling of the houseboat. There was an attraction about his whole being that was irresistible. He was a true symbol of resistance in the face of death. That was why Anis liked talking to him so much, in spite of their acquaintance of barely a month.

Anis rose and took his place at the table. He began to eat a chop, holding it in his fingers. He gazed at the wooden partition, painted with sky-blue distemper. He

followed the progress of a small gecko as it scuttled across
the partition to secrete itself behind a light switch. The
gecko reminded him of the Head of Department. Why
was that? A sudden question plagued him. Did the Fa-
timid Caliph Mu'izz li-Din Illah have any living descen-
dants who might one day rise to claim the throne of
Cairo as their own? "How old are you, Amm Abduh?"
he asked.

Amm Abduh was standing behind the folding screen
that concealed the outer door, and looking down at him
from above like a cypress tree towering among the clouds.
He smiled, as if he had not taken the question seriously.
"How old am I?"

Anis nodded, licking his lips.

The old man spoke again. "Who knows?"

I am no expert when it comes to guessing ages, but
more than likely he was walking the earth before a single
tree was planted along this street. He is still so strong,
given his age, that one can hardly believe it. He looks
after the big floats under the houseboat, and pulls the
boat on a rope to a new berth whenever it is necessary,
and it follows him obediently; he waters the plants, he
leads the prayer, and he is a good cook.

"Have you always lived alone in that hut?" Anis continued.

"There's only just enough room for me on my own!"

"Where did you come from, Amm Abduh?" he asked
next, but the old man merely said: "Ah!"

"Don't you have relatives in Cairo?"

"No one."

"We have that in common at least . . . You are an excellent cook, by the way."

"Thank you."

"And you eat more than is good for someone of your age."

"I eat what I can digest."

Anis contemplated the remains of the chop. One day, all that would be left of the Head of Department would be bones like those. How he would love to see him being called to account on Judgment Day! He began to peel a banana, and continued his inquiries. "When did you come to work on the houseboat?"

"When they brought it to this berth."

"When was that?"

"Oh . . ."

"And does it have the same owner now as it did then?"

"There has been one owner after another here."

"And do you like your job?"

"I *am* the houseboat!" Amm Abduh replied proudly. "Because I am the ropes and floats, and if I forgot my duties for a minute it would sink or be carried away by the current!"

His simple pride was appealing. Anis chuckled, and gazed at him for a moment before asking: "What is the most important thing in the world?"

"To be hale and hearty."

There was something mysterious and magical about his reply that made Anis laugh for a long time. Then he asked: "When was the last time you loved a woman?"

"Well!"

"Have you found nothing else to make you happy, after love?"

"Prayer is my comfort now."

"Your voice is beautiful when you call them to prayer," Anis remarked, and then he added merrily: "Even so, you're not too holy to go and fetch the kif, or bring back one of the street girls for us!"

Amm Abduh guffawed, throwing back his head with its white skullcap. He did not reply.

"Isn't that so?"

Amm Abduh passed one big hand over his face. "I serve the gentlemen," he said simply.

But no. No, it was not just that. He was the houseboat, as he had said. The ropes and floats, the plants, the food, the women, the prayers.

Taking a towel, Anis went through a side door to wash his hands at the basin, and came back, saying to himself that it was due to excess alone that most of the Caliphs had not lived long. He saw Amm Abduh busily wiping the table, his back bent like a bowed palm tree. Playfully, he asked him: "Have you ever seen a ghost?"

"I've seen everything," Amm Abduh replied.

Anis winked. "So there has never been a good family living on this houseboat?" he asked.

"Hmm!"

"O guardian of our pleasures! If you did not like this life, you would have left it on the first day!"

"How could I, when I built the mosque with my own hands?"

Anis looked now at the books on the shelves, which

covered the whole of the long wall to the left of the door. It was a library of history, from the dawn of time to the atomic age, domain of his imagination and storehouse of his dreams. At random, he took down a book on monasticism in the Coptic period in order to read, as he did every day, for an hour or two before his siesta. Amm Abduh finished his work, and came to ask if Anis wanted anything else before he left.

"What is going on outside, Amm Abduh?" Anis asked him.

"The same as usual, sir."

"Nothing new?"

"Why don't you go out, sir?"

"I go to the Ministry every day."

"I mean, for relaxation."

Anis laughed. "My eyes look inward, not outward like the rest of God's servants!" And he dismissed Amm Abduh, telling him to wake him if he was still asleep at sunset.

3

Everything was ready. The mattresses were arranged in a large semicircle just inside the door to the balcony. On a brass tray in the middle of the semicircle stood the water pipe and the brazier for the charcoal. Dusk came down over the trees and the water, and a clement calm reigned. Homecoming flocks of white doves flew swiftly over the Nile.

Anis sat cross-legged behind the tray, staring out at the sunset with his customary sleepy gaze—sleepy, that is, until the lump of kif, dissolved in the bitter black coffee, worked its magic. Then things would change. Abstract, cubist, surrealist, fauvist forms would take the place of the evergreen and guava and acacia trees and the girls on the other houseboats; and humankind would return to the primeval age of mosses . . . What could it have been that had turned a whole band of Egyptians into monks?

And what was that last joke he had heard, the one about the monk and the cobbler?

The houseboat shook faintly; there were footsteps on the gangway. He prepared to greet the newcomer. It was a girl of medium build, with golden hair. She came out onto the balcony, greeting him gaily.

"I bid a welcome to the Ministry of Foreign Affairs!" he murmured in reply.

Layla Zaydan had been a friend for the past ten years. She was thirty-five and unmarried, which was appropriate for one of the first explorers of the space of female liberty; one, moreover, who had set out from a bastion of conservatism. You have not touched her, Anis, but age has. Look at those wrinkles as light as down at the corners of her eyes and mouth, and that tinge of dryness, harsh and bleak, like a water jar long since drained. There was still a desirable beauty in her clear skin, in spite of a thickness to the tip of her nose, and in spite of something obscure, something encroaching on her which threatened her ruin. In the age of Cheops she was a shepherdess in the Sinai, but died, bitten by a blind snake, leaving no trace . . .

She did not turn to him as she spoke. She seemed to be addressing the Nile. "I had a hard day at the Ministry. I translated twenty pages of foolscap."

"And how is our foreign policy today?"

"What do you expect?"

"Oh, all I want is a quiet life. Quiet and respectable . . ."

She left the balcony for the farthest mattress on the right-hand side, where she sat down. "It's the same scene as ever," she said. "Amm Abduh is sitting in the garden like a statue, and here you are, filling the pipe."

"That is because Man has to work."

He yielded to a reeling sensation. The evening seemed personified, a wanton creature, one who had lived for millions of years. He began to talk, in a roundabout way, about a woman who he said was the slave of love; whenever one lover deserted her, he said, she threw herself into the arms of another. He added that such behavior could be explained by the waxing and waning of the moon.

Layla smiled coldly. Copying his previous ironic tone, she said: "And that's because Woman has to love!"

And then she grumbled: "Wretched man!" and he detected in her face the faint warnings of anger, but no trace of real antipathy. He was sure that when it came to jokes she was no Queen Victoria, ruler of an age bound by convention.

"Why don't you take me as your lover?" he suggested, not particularly seriously.

When he continued to look at her, she answered: "If one day you ever used the word 'love' as the subject of a sentence," she said, "you would never remember what the predicate was. Ever."

He recalled how good he was at Arabic, as good as the Head of Department; witness the man's decision to cut two days' pay from his salary, for no reason except that he had written a blank page. And he remembered also how Layla had said to him once: "You have no heart." One night it was, when all the friends had gone and only Khalid Azzuz and Layla remained on the house-boat. And without any preliminary Anis had grasped her arm and said: "You are mine tonight." Why did it always have to be Khalid? Khalid who inherited you after Ragab left you! And so, for me, only the night is mine. His voice had been raised in anger that night, raised against the dawn prayer. Amm Abduh outside, calling to prayer, you yourself yelling like a madman inside; and Khalid, spreading his hands wide in supplication, and saying: "You've made a scandal of us!"

Layla had laughed at first, and then cried. She had raised a highly philosophical question. For she loved Khalid, and on account of that could not give in to Anis, in spite of their friendship—if she did, she would be a whore. And he had shouted that night that the call to prayer was easier to understand than these riddles!

"Friendship is more important," Layla pleaded now, to clear the air. "Friendship is for life."

"May God grant you a long one, then."

He filled the pipe so that they could smoke together while waiting for the others. She took a greedy puff and coughed for a long time. And he said again what he usually said, that the first pull on the pipe made you cough; it was after that that the pleasure came. And he thought to himself that it was not so strange that the Egyptians had worshipped the Pharaoh; what was extraordinary was that the Pharaoh had believed himself to be a god . . .

The houseboat shook, more violently this time, and a hubbub of voices came from outside. He glanced toward the doorway concealed by the screen and saw a lively group of companions follow one another in: Ahmad Nasr, Mustafa Rashid, Ali al-Sayyid, and Khalid Azzuz . . . "Good evening . . . Good evening to you!" Khalid sat down next to Layla; as for Ali al-Sayyid, he threw himself down to the right of Anis, crying: "Come to our aid!" So Anis set about filling the pipe and stacking glowing pieces of charcoal on top, and the water pipe was soon being passed around the circle. "Any news of Ragab?" Mustafa Rashid inquired.

Anis told him that Ragab had telephoned to say that he was in the studio, and that he would come as soon as he had finished work.

A breeze blowing in from the balcony made the coals glow on the brazier. Anis was now as animated as he would become. His broad face suffused with a profound rapture, he announced that whoever it was who had made a magnificent tomb out of human history, a tomb that graced the shelves of every library, had not begrudged them a few moments of pleasure.

Khalid Azzuz looked toward Ali al-Sayyid. "So does the press have any news?" he asked.

Ali indicated Layla with a lift of his chin. "The Ministry of Foreign Affairs is here before you."

"But I heard the most astonishing facts . . ."

"Don't bother our brains with it," Anis said cynically. "Whatever else we get to hear, this world of ours will still be here, the same as ever it was, absolutely nothing happening at all."

Mustafa Rashid cleared his throat. "And what's more," he said, "the world does not concern us any more than we concern it. In any way at all."

Anis agreed. "As long as the pipe is still being passed around, what does it matter to you?"

Khalid regarded him, delighted. "Wisdom," he said, "from the mouth of the intoxicated!"

"Let me tell you what happened to me today with

the Director General," Anis continued, and the story of the pen provoked a storm of laughter. "Pens like that are used to sign peace treaties," Ali said finally.

The water pipe continued on its glowing, melodious way. A halo of midges clustered around the neon light. Outside, beyond the balcony, darkness had set in. The Nile had vanished save for a few geometric shapes, some regular, some irregular: the reflections of the streetlights on the opposite bank, and the illuminated windows of the other houseboats. The Director's bald pate loomed, like the hull of an upturned boat, in the embrace of darkness. He must surely be a scion of the Hyksos kings, and one day would return to the desert . . . The worst thing Anis had to fear was that the evening would come to an end like the youth of Layla Zaydan, like the gray ash encroaching on the heart of the embers . . .

Who was it who had said that revolutions are plotted by the clever, fought by the brave, and profited from by cowards?

Amm Abduh came and took the pipe away to change the water. Then he brought it back and left again without uttering a word. Khalid Azzuz wiped his gold-rimmed spectacles, declaring his admiration for the old man. Ahmad Nasr broke his customary silence. "A man from the stock of dinosaurs," he said.

"We should thank God that he's past his prime," added Mustafa Rashid. "Otherwise there wouldn't be a single woman left for us!"

Anis related the conversation he had had with the old man.

"The world needs a giant like him to solve its political problems," said Ali.

The pipe gurgled louder in the momentary silence that followed. From outside came the croaking of frogs and the chirp of crickets. Through the spreading veil of smoke, Layla's hand crept into Khalid's; friends of a lifetime, a solace to one another. Ahmad's long, hooked nose was rivaled only by Ali's—though the latter was set in a wider, paler face. Beyond the balcony the darkness spoke, and said: *Concern yourself with nothing.* Borne down on the rays of a dull red star, it had come, across a hundred million light-years, to reach the smoking party. *Do not make your life a burden,* it said. *Even the Director General will one day be gone, as was the ink from your pen.* And there was no care left now in his heart, not since they committed his precious ones to the ground . . . If you really want to perpetrate some piece of idiocy, to make people stare, then strip off your clothes and prance around in Opera Square—where you will find the statue of Ibrahim Pasha on his charger, pointing at the Continental Hotel. Which must be the most bizarre advertisement for tourism in the entire country . . .

"Is it true that we will die someday?"

"Wait until it's broadcast on the news."

"Anis Zaki is philosophizing!"

"And he's brought up something new this time!"

"What was that last joke?" Layla wondered.

"There are no jokes anymore," Mustafa replied. "Not now that our lives have become a sick joke."

Anis gazed out into the darkness beyond the balcony. He saw a huge whale quietly approaching the houseboat. It was not the strangest thing he had seen under cover of night, true; but now it gaped as if intending to swallow the houseboat whole. The conversation went back and forth among the smokers regardless, and so he decided to wait, likewise regardless, and see what happened. The whale came no closer; and then it winked, saying: *I am the whale that saved Jonah.* And then it retreated—and vanished. Anis laughed, and Layla asked him what he was laughing at.

"Strange apparitions," he replied.

"So why don't we see them?"

He replied, still busy with the water pipe: "As the great sheikh says: 'He who turns this way and that will arrive at nothing.' "

An unrestrained volley of expostulations followed. "No sheikhs here, you old fraud!"

"Who can tell for sure where the next earthquake will strike!"

"And even so, there's singing and dancing everywhere."

"If you wanted to have a really good laugh, then why not look at the earth from above."

"Lucky they who look down from above."

"Although when the new finance bill comes into force, all our minds will be at rest."

"Does the bill apply to animals as well?"

"I fear it applies primarily to animals . . ."

"We could always emigrate to the moon."

"You know what I'm afraid of? That God is sick of us."

"Like everything is sick of everything else."

"Like Ragab is sick of his sweethearts."

"Like being sick of it is sick of being sick of it."

"And the solution, is there no solution?"

"Yes indeed—that we all pull together and change the world!"

"Or we stay as we are, which is better—more long-lasting, you see."

The houseboat shook at the approach of footsteps. They waited for Ragab to appear, but instead there came in a gay, lively woman whose plump figure had one fault only, which was that her bust was a little fuller than her hips. Saniya Kamil! She kissed everyone in greeting, meeting their gaze with gray eyes. Ali al-Sayyid offered her the seat next to him. "We haven't seen you since last Ramadan!" he said. He kissed her hand twice. "A passing visit?"

"A visit for always!" she replied.

"That means that your husband has left you!"

"Or that I have left him," she said, taking the water pipe.

She puffed voraciously and said, to satisfy the curiosity around her: "I caught him flirting with the new neighbor!"

"Salacious news!"

"And I should think they heard me on the seventh floor!"

"Bravo!"

"So I left the house and the children and went to my mother in Maadi."

"That is a shame—but necessary, for the renewal of married life."

"And the first idea that came into my head was to come and visit my houseboat here!"

"Absolutely right! An eye for an eye!"

Mustafa indicated Ali. "Now's the time for the emergency husband!" he said to Saniya.

"Why can't it be my turn this time?" Anis demanded heatedly.

Ali humored him. "I've always been Saniya's standby, for a long time now—"

"And I—"

"You are our lord, and the jewel in our crown, and the master of our pleasures; and if you were ever to bother with love, you could have all you wanted and more . . ."

"Liar."

Ali pointed to the water pipe. "Anyway, you've no time for love!"

"Bastards! Let me tell you the story of what happened with the Director General."

"But you have recounted every detail. Have you forgotten, master of pleasure?"

"Damn you all! Your lives will be over before you get the message!"

The water pipe circulated, favoring Saniya, who had not smoked since Ramadan. She's dark, nervous, likes to laugh, thought Anis. And she never forgets her children even in the intoxication of love and kif. She will go back to her husband in the end. But she will live with him one year and leave him the next, swearing always that it is his fault. Ragab brought her the first time, just as he had brought Layla, for he is the god of sex, the provider of women for our boat. I knew an ancient forebear of his who walked the forests before one house was built on the face of the earth, who in the arms of women would bury his fears of animals and darkness and the unknown and death. Who had a radar in his eyes and a radio in his ears and a grenade for a fist. Who achieved extraordinary victories before expiring exhausted. And as for his great-grandson, Ragab . . .

The houseboat shook. Ragab al-Qadi's voice could be heard. He was talking to someone with him. "Watch your step, my dear," he was saying.

Their faces were filled with anticipation. "Perhaps an actress from the studio," murmured Khalid.

Ragab appeared from behind the screen by the door. He was slender, dark, and fine-featured—and preceded by a teenage girl. She was also dark, with small regular features in a round, shallow-looking face. Ragab had clearly noticed his friends' surprise at her extreme youth. Smiling, he announced in a melodious voice: "This is Miss Sana al-Rashidi, a student at the Faculty of Arts."

4 ❧

All eyes were fixed on the newcomer, who remained unperturbed and met their gazes with a bold smile.

Ragab put his arm around her waist and led her to sit beside him. "Rescue me, master of pleasures!" he said.

"In front of Mademoiselle?" Ahmad queried.

Ragab reproached him. "There's no need for pretense," he said. "Not with such a sincere admirer!"

He took a long, deep drag on the pipe, so that the charcoal on the tobacco glowed and sent up a dancing tongue of flame. He closed his eyes in gratification, and then opened them to say: "Let me introduce you to the friends who from this night on will be your family."

Then he realized for the first time that Saniya Kamil was there. He shook her hand warmly and guessed the reason for her coming, and she agreed, laughing, that he was right. He introduced her to Sana.

"Saniya Kamil, graduate of the Mère de Dieu College, wife and mother. A truly excellent woman, who in times of domestic distress returns to her old friends. A lady with great experience of womanhood, as single girl, wife, and mother—a fund of wisdom for the young girls on our houseboat."

Involuntary sounds of mirth. Sana smiled. Saniya gave Ragab a cold, but not angry glance. Ragab turned to Layla.

"Miss Layla Zaydan, graduate of the American University, a translator at the Ministry of Foreign Affairs. There is no one more beautiful or cultured than she, not in the whole history of female advancement in this country. Oh, by the way, her hair really is that golden color; it's not a wig, or dyed."

Then he turned his attention to Anis, absorbed in his work. "Anis Zaki, civil servant in the Ministry of Health, and the company's master of ceremonies and Minister for Pipe-Smoking Affairs. A man as cultured as your good self—this is his library—who has made the rounds of the Medicine, Science, and Law faculties, each time departing—like any good man unconcerned with appearances—with knowledge and not qualifications. He is from a respectable country family, but has lived alone in Cairo for a long time; he is quite a cosmopolitan now. Don't take his silence amiss—he seldom speaks, roaming as he does in another realm entirely."

Ahmad was the next to be introduced. "Ahmad Nasr, Director of Accounts at the Ministry of Social Affairs. A civil servant of note, expert in a great number of matters—selling, buying, and many other things of a practical and useful nature. He has a daughter your age, Sana, but he is an exceptional husband, worthy of attention. Imagine—he has been married for twenty years and has never once deceived his wife. Her company does not bore him; in fact, his attachment to married life grows stronger. He should be a case study at the next medical conference."

Ragab continued, indicating Mustafa now. "Mustafa Rashid, the well-known lawyer. Successful advocate and

There is nothing to fear as long as the whale remains in the water. The hand of this underage girl is as small as Napoleon's, but her nails are red and as pointed as the prow of a racing skiff. Now that she is here, we have broken every rule in the book . . .

Thus the darkness spoke.

Mustafa coughed. "And which of the arts does Mademoiselle specialize in?"

"History," she replied, her voice coy and girlish.

"Marvelous!" cried Anis.

Ragab rebuked him. "Not your gory type of history! Her history is concerned with nice things!"

"There are no nice things in history."

"What about the passion of Antony and Cleopatra?"

"That was a gory passion."

"But one not wholly confined to swords and asps."

Sana appeared uneasy. She looked toward the screened door and asked: "Aren't you afraid of the police?"

Mustafa smiled. "The arts police?"

After the laughter died down, she said: "Or being investigated?"

"Because we are afraid of the police and the army," Ali said, "and the English and the Americans, and the visible and the invisible, we have reached the point where we're not afraid of anything!"

"But the door is open!"

"Amm Abduh is outside, and he can be counted upon to turn away any intruders."

Ragab smiled. "Forget your worries, light of my

philosopher as well, married to an inspector in the Ministry of Education. He searches earnestly for the Absolute, and no doubt he will succeed in finding it one of these nights. But beware of him, my dear, for he says that to this day he has not found the perfect ideal of womanhood . . ."

Ragab then gave Ali a pat on the back. "Ali al-Sayyid, the famous art critic. Of course, you have read his work. I have the pleasure of informing you that he dreams of an ideal city, an imaginary one. As for the reality, he has two wives, and is also the close friend of Saniya Kamil, not to mention anything else . . ."

Lastly, Ragab indicated Khalid. "Khalid Azzuz, a member of the first rank of short-story writers. He owns an apartment block and a villa and a car, and several shares in the theory of art for art's sake, plus a son and daughter; and he also has a personal philosophy which I am not sure how to name—but certainly promiscuity is among its external traits . . ."

He smiled at them all, revealing regular white teeth. "There remains only Amm Abduh," he murmured, "whose ghostly form we passed in the garden on our way here. You will meet him in due course. Everyone in the street knows him."

Anis called Amm Abduh and asked him to change the water in the pipe. He took it away through the side door and returned it in a moment, and then went away again. Sana's eyes widened in amazement at the towering figure. Ragab said: "Luckily he's the soul of obedience. He could drown us any time he wanted."

eyes," he said to the girl. "The economic plan is keeping everyone busy. The authorities have enough to do already without bothering with the likes of us."

Mustafa Rashid offered her the pipe. "Try this kind of courage," he suggested.

But she declined gently. "One step at a time," Ragab said. "Bare hands came before space technology. Roll her a joint."

In two minutes the cigarette was proffered. She took it rather cautiously, and fixed it between her lips. Ahmad looked at her sympathetically. He is afraid for his own daughter, thought Anis. And if my daughter had lived, she would be Sana's double.

But what is the point, whether you remain on this earth or depart? Or whether you live as long as the turtle? Since historical time is nothing compared to the time of the cosmos, Sana is really a contemporary of Eve. One day the Nile's waters will bring us something new, something which it would be better we did not name. The voice of the darkness spoke to him: *Well said.*

And I believe that I may well hear, one night, the same voice command me to do some extraordinary thing—something to bewilder those who do not believe in miracles. The scientists have had their say on the stars, but what are the stars, in fact, but single worlds that chose solitude, worlds separated one from the other by thousands of light-years? Whatever or whoever you are, do something, for the Nothing has crushed us . . .

"So do you find time to study?" Ahmad asked Sana kindly.

Ragab replied for her. "Of course—but she's crazy about art as well."

The girl shook her finger at him. "Don't make me the entire subject of your conversation!"

"Perish the thought!"

"Do you want to be an actress?" Ahmad continued. When Sana smiled and did not demur, he continued: "But . . ."

Ragab interrupted him. "Quiet, you reactionary— and I don't use that disgusting term lightly." He took Sana's chin between finger and thumb and tilted her head toward him. Then he said, examining her carefully: "Let me study your face . . . beautiful, that fresh bloom harboring a hidden power. A sugared date with a hard kernel; the gaze of a young girl—which, when she frowns, radiates the subtlety of a woman! Which role would fit you? Perhaps the part of the girl in *The Mystery of the Lake*."

She was intrigued. "What part is that, exactly?"

"She is a bedouin girl who loves a wily fisherman— one of those men who make a game out of love. He scorns her at first, but she tames him eventually. By the end he is wrapped around her little finger."

"Could I really play that?"

"I am talking about an artistic instinct," Ragab replied. "One that producers and distributors alike believe in. Just a minute—pucker your lips. Show me how you kiss. Beware of being embarrassed. Embarrassment is the enemy of the art of acting. Now, in front of everyone, a real kiss, real in every sense of the word. A kiss after

which the international situation must surely im-
prove . . ."

He put his long, strong arms around her, and their
lips met with force and warmth, in a silence unbroken
even by the gurgling of the pipe. Then Mustafa Rashid
cried: "That was a glimpse of the Absolute I've been
wearing myself out trying to find!"

"Maestro and maestra!" Khalid gushed. "My congratulations! Indeed, we must all congratulate ourselves;
we must salute this splendid moment of civilization. Now
we can say that Fascism has been completely routed!
That Euclid's axioms have been demolished! Sana—no
surnames from now on—please accept my sincere ac-
claim . . ."

Layla smiled. "For goodness' sake," she said, "let
someone else speak."

"Jealousy is not an instinct, as the ignorant maintain," Khalid said ruefully. "It is the legacy of feudal-
ism."

I am not a whore. Damnation! Oh, smell of the Nile,
heavy with the scent of a dusty, exhausting journey.
There is an ancient tree in Brazil that stood on the earth
before the Pyramids existed. Am I alone among these
drugged minds to laugh in the face of this unstoppable
turn in history's tide? Am I alone when it whispers in
my ear that forty knocks on the door will make the
impossible come true? When will I play football with the
planets? One day long ago I was forced into a bloody
battle, and I alone am keeping the adversaries apart . . .

Outside, beyond the balcony, a bat sped past like a

bullet. Anis contemplated the decorations on the brass tray, interlinking circles separated by gold and silver spangles, now veiled by ash and scraps of tobacco. For a while he dozed, insensible, where he sat, and when he opened his eyes he found that Mustafa Rashid and Ahmad Nasr had gone. The door of the room overlooking the garden was closed on Layla and Khalid; and Saniya and Ali were in the middle room. As for Ragab and Sana, they were standing out on the balcony, murmuring to each other. The only room left empty was his own, and more than likely his door as well would be shut in his face that night.

The lovers were talking.

"Certainly not!"

" 'Certainly not'? That's not a very suitable reply, considering the age we live in."

"I should be studying with a girlfriend."

"Well, let it be study with a boyfriend."

Anis stretched out his leg and knocked against the water pipe. It toppled over, and the black spittle poured out and spread toward the threshold of the balcony.

There was no importance to anything. Even rest had no meaning. And Man had invented nothing more sincere than farce.

Then Amm Abduh's great height was blocking the light from the midge-surrounded lamp.

"Is it time?" the old man asked.

"Yes."

Amm Abduh began to collect the things and sweep up the scraps with great care. Then he looked at Anis. "When will you go to your room?"

"There is a new bride in there . . ."

"Ah!"

"Don't you like it?"

Amm Abduh laughed. "The street girls are nicer—and cheaper."

Anis roared with laughter. His voice rang out over the surface of the Nile. "You ignorant old man," he said. "Do you think these women are like those girls?"

"Have they got more legs, then?"

"Of course not, but they are respectable ladies!"

"Ah!"

"They don't sell themselves. They give and take, just like men."

"Ah!"

"Ah!" Anis mimicked.

"So will you sleep out on the balcony until the dew comes to wash your face?" Amm Abduh asked; and he saluted him as he left, announcing that he was going to give the call to the dawn prayer.

Anis looked at the stars. He began to count as many as he could. The counting exhausted him . . . and then a breeze came scented from the palace gardens. The Caliph Harun al-Rashid was sitting on a couch under an apricot tree, and the courtesans were dallying around him. You were pouring him some wine from a golden jug. The Caliph, the Commander of the Faithful, became finer and finer until he was more transparent than the wind. "Bring me what you have there!" he said to you.

But you had nothing with you, so you said that you were already dead. But then the servant girl plucked the strings of her lute and sang:

"I recall the days of love's fever,
Bent o'er my heart for fear it will break
Gone are love's evenings forever,
Let the tears then fall from your eyes . . ."

Harun al-Rashid was so transported that he tapped his hands and feet, and you said: Now is your chance, and slipped lightly away; but the giant guard saw you and came toward you; and you ran, and he ran after you, unsheathing his sword, and you screamed, calling for help to the Family of the Prophet; and he swore that they would put you in the prison of the palace . . .

5 ≈

Refreshed by a cold shower, Anis gave himself up to the sunset. A somnolent, all-pervasive calm reigned. Flocks of pigeons made a white horizon over the Nile. If he could only invite the Director General to the houseboat, then he would be guaranteed a life as peaceful as the sunset, free of its present rankling thorns. He sipped the last of the bitter black coffee. He had mixed a little magic into it, and now he licked out the dregs with his tongue.

The friends arrived all together—as did Ragab and Sana. They had been inseparable all week, and Sana had finally become acquainted with the water pipe—at which Ahmad Nasr had whispered in Ragab's ear, "She's a minor!" And Ragab had whispered back, propping his elbow on Anis' knee: "I'm not the first artist in her life!" And Layla Zaydan had pronounced: "Woe betide those who respect love in an age when love has no respect!"

Ahmad found no one to whom he could expound his conservative ideas—save the peaceable Anis, to whom he said, leaning toward him: "Wonderful, the way yesterday's whore becomes today's philosopher!"

"That," replied Anis, "is the way it usually goes with philosophy."

Then Ali al-Sayyid snapped his fingers, causing heads to turn toward him. "By the way," he began in a serious tone, "I have a message to relay, before you all become too addled."

When he had the attention of some of the company, he continued in a clear voice: "Samara Bahgat wishes to visit the houseboat!"

Now the interest was universal. All eyes were fixed upon him, including those of Anis, though he continued to minister to the water pipe.

"The journalist?"

"The same. My beautiful and renowned colleague."

A silence fell while this news was digested. Unreadable glances were exchanged. "But why does she want to visit us?" Ahmad inquired finally.

"I am the one who has made her interested in you. We've had many long conversations about the houseboat."

"You've got a loose tongue," Ragab remarked. "But does your friend *like* houseboats?"

"It's not so much whether she does or not—more that she knows, or has heard, about more than one person here. Myself, being a colleague and friend, and Khalid Azzuz because of his stories, and you from your films—"

"Does she have any idea of what goes on here?"

"I think so. She is not completely unfamiliar with our world, because of her work, and her general experience of life."

"If we are to judge her on the strength of what she writes, then she is an alarmingly serious person," Ragab said.

"Well, she is serious. But everyone has a taste for the more mundane side of life."

"And has she made other excursions like this?" Ahmad asked, with some irritation.

"I should imagine so. She's a friendly person, she likes people."

"But she'll constrain us," Ahmad pursued.

"No, no, no. Don't have any worries about that."

"So will she—participate?"

"To a certain extent—in our more blameless activities, that is."

"Blameless! So we *are* going to be investigated, then!"

Ali stressed that she was coming for no other purpose than to get to know them.

Concern yourself no more with the matter, or else all the water pipe's good will come to nothing. Remember how the Persians received the first news of the Arab conquest . . . Anis smiled. He spotted a number of dead midges on the brass tray, which prompted him to ask: "What class of animal do midges belong to?"

The question held up the flow of their ideas in an annoying and intrusive way. "Mammals," Mustafa Rashid replied sarcastically.

"The messenger's only duty is to deliver the message," Ali went on. "If you don't like the idea . . ."

Ragab interrupted him. "We have not heard the opinion of the ladies."

Layla raised no objection. Neither did Saniya. As for Sana, she suggested that Anis and Ahmad and Mustafa should be allowed to decide, "since they are the ones who need girlfriends!"

"No—no," protested Ali, "what an unthinkable idea—don't embarrass me, please!"

"But in that case," wondered Sana, pushing back a stray lock of hair from her brow, "why do you want her to come?"

"I have nothing to add!"

"If the midge is a mammal"—Anis pursued his train of thought—"how can we maintain that your friend is not in the same class?"

Ali addressed everyone, ignoring Anis' interruption. "Your freedom is guaranteed in every way. You can say or do what you like—smoke, tell your ribald jokes; there will be no investigations, no probes, no reporter's trickery of any kind. You can rest assured. But it would not do for you to treat her as a frivolous woman."

"*Frivolous* woman?"

"What I mean is that she is an excellent person, just like any of you, who should not be treated as if she were . . . loose."

"Really," said Ahmad, "I don't understand anything."

"That is to be expected of you, O Nineteenth Century personified. Everyone else understands me without any difficulty at all."

"Perhaps," said Khalid, "in spite of those articles of hers, she's actually an unreformed bourgeoise."

"She is not bourgeois in any sense of the word."

"Why don't you tell us something about her," Mustafa suggested. "That would be more useful."

"Certainly. She's twenty-five. She graduated in English just before she turned twenty. She's an excellent journalist, better by far than most people her age. And she has ambitions in the artistic sphere which she hopes to realize one day. She looks at life from a serious angle, but she is very pleasant company. Everybody knows that she refused to marry a very well-to-do bourgeois man, in spite of her small salary."

"Why?"

"The man was under forty, the director of a firm, the owner of an apartment block—like Khalid here—and a relation on her father's side to boot. But, as I understand it, she did not love him . . ."

"If we can judge by her heart, then," said Khalid, "she's a radical."

"Call her progressive, if you like. But genuine and sincere as well."

"Has she ever been arrested?"

"No. I have known her as a colleague ever since she got her first job on *Kulli Shay'* magazine."

"Perhaps when she was a student, then?"

"I think not, or else I would have found out about it during our long talks together. In any case, it wouldn't influence my opinion of her one way or the other."

Sana spoke. "Why do you want to invite such a dangerous woman to the houseboat," she asked, "when she can't entertain us in the least?"

"She must come," said Layla. "We need some new blood here."

"Make a decision," said Ali. "She's at the club now. If you like, I can call her on the telephone and ask her to come over."

"Did you tell her that it is the whale who gathers us all here?" Anis asked him.

Ali did not reply. He suggested taking a vote. Anis laughed at his own embalmed memories. He suggested that they bring Amm Abduh to add his vote as well. Ragab put his arm around Sana, and Ali rose to go to the telephone.

6 ❧

Half an hour after his telephone call, Ali al-Sayyid left his seat in order to be ready to welcome the newcomer at the door. Not long afterward, they felt the faint vibration of footsteps on the gangway. Ahmad wished aloud that they had hidden the water pipe so that they could feel easy in the presence of the visitor, but Ragab signaled contemptuously to Anis. "Pile it on," he said.

She appeared smiling from behind the screen, and came forward—followed by Ali—to meet their combined gazes in a calm, friendly, and unembarrassed way. All the men rose to their feet. Even Anis stood up, his white robe rumpled up over his shins. Ali began the conventional introductions. Ahmad offered to bring her a chair, but she preferred to sit on a mattress; and Ragab—involuntarily—moved closer to Sana in order to make room for her. Anis resumed his work, stealing occasional glances at her. He had been led, by what he had heard, to expect someone rather odd, and she was definitely a woman of character; but she was also quite charmingly feminine. From under drooping lids he saw that her dark complexion was undisguised by makeup. Her features were as open as her simple elegance, but in her gaze there was an intelligence that prevented him from fathoming her. He imagined that he had seen her before, but in what bygone age? Had she been queen or subject? Another furtive glance—but this time she showed him a new picture! He tried to absorb it all, but the concentration tired him out and he turned away to the Nile instead.

The customary hubbub of introductions and compliments was followed by a silence. The gurgle of the water pipe made a duet with the crickets. Adroitly, Samara avoided looking at the pipe in any meaningful way. When Anis passed her the mouthpiece she put it to her lips without smoking, by way of salutation, and then passed it to Ragab, who took it, saying: "Be at your ease."

She turned to him. "I saw you in your last film, *Tree Without Fruit,*" she said. "I can say that you played your part extraordinarily well."

He was not so modest as to be embarrassed by praise. "Opinion, or flattery?" he asked warily.

"Opinion, of course—and one shared by millions!"

Anis looked through the smoke at Sana and, seeing her tame her rebellious lock of hair, smiled. The Director General himself, with all the power conferred on him by financial and administrative directives, could not control all "incomings and outgoings." Thousands of comets, scattered by stars, burned and frittered away as they were flung into the earth's atmosphere, and not one of them found their way into the archives. Nor were they entered in the register of incoming mail. As for pain, that was the heart's domain only . . .

Now Samara was addressing Khalid Azzuz. "The last story of yours that I read was the tale of the piper . . ."

Khalid adjusted his spectacles.

"The piper whose pipe turned into a serpent!" she continued.

"And since its publication," said Mustafa, "he well deserves the epithet of 'python.'"

"It's a strange, exciting story," she said.

"Our friend is a leading light of the old school—the school of 'art for art's sake,'" said Ali. "Don't expect anything else from this houseboat!"

"Oh, I think it won't be long before the theater of the irrational, known generally as the absurd, will be founded here," said Mustafa.

"But the absurd has existed among us in abundance, even before it became an art," said Ragab. "Your colleague Ali al-Sayyid is known for his absurd dreams, and Mustafa Rashid strives after the absurd in its guise of Absolute. And our master of ceremonies here—his whole life, since he cut himself off from the world some twenty years ago, is absurd."

Samara laughed aloud, throwing off her gravity. "I am really a wisewoman, then!" she said. "My heart told me that I would find wonderful and interesting things among you!"

"Was it your heart that told you," wondered Ragab, "or Ali's tattle?"

"He said nothing but good!"

"But our houseboat is not unique, surely?"

"Perhaps not, but the more people there are, the fewer who can live in friendship."

"I never imagined that I would hear a journalist say that!"

"People generally present the same face to us as they do to the camera."

"Have we not met you in a sincere and guileless way?" said Khalid. "When will you give to us in kind?"

She laughed. "Consider that I have. Or give me a little time."

Anis piled the brazier with charcoal and carried it to the threshold of the balcony, where it was exposed to the breeze. He waited. The patches of heat grew gradually larger until the black charcoal had turned a soft, deep, glowing, crumbling red. Dozens of small tongues of flame darted up, branded with evening glow, and began to spread so that they joined into a dancing wave, pure and transparent, crowned at the tips with a spectral blue. Then the charcoal crackled, and swarms of spark clusters flew up. Female voices screamed, and he returned the brazier to its place. He acknowledged to himself his unlimited wonder at fire. It was more beautiful than roses or green grass or violet dawn; how could it conceal within its heart such a great destructive power? If you feel inclined, you should tell them the story of the person who discovered fire. That old friend who had a nose like Ali's, and Ragab's charisma, and the giant stature of Amm Abduh . . . Where had that curious notion gone? He had been about to toss it into the discussion when he was carrying the brazier out to the balcony . . .

"I am a lawyer," Mustafa was saying. "And lawyers by their nature think the worst. I can almost imagine what is going through your head about us now!"

"There is nothing like that in my head!"

"Your articles pour forth bitter criticism of nihilism, and we could be considered—in the eyes of some—nihilism itself!"

"No, no," she replied. "One cannot judge people on what they do in their free time."

Ragab laughed. "Better to say 'free lifetimes'!"

"Don't remind me that I'm stranger to you," Samara said to him.

"It is bad manners to talk like this about ourselves!" Ahmad said. "We should really be finding out about you."

"I am not a mystery!" she said.

"The writer's articles can generally be counted on to reveal the writer," said Ali.

"Like your critical pieces, you mean?" asked Mustafa.

The room resounded with laughter. Even Ali laughed for a long time. Finally he said, his face still full of mirth: "I am one of you, O dissolutes of our time, and whoever is like his friends has done no wrong. But unfortunately this girl is sincere."

"Everyone is writing about socialism," remarked Khalid, "while most writers dream of acquiring a fortune, and of nights full of dazzling society."

"Do you discuss these matters a great deal?" Samara asked.

"No, but we are forced to if someone alludes to the way we live."

Anis called Amm Abduh. The huge old man came in and took the pipe out through the side door, and then brought it back after changing the water.

Samara's eyes were drawn to him all the while he

was in the room. After he had gone, she murmured:
"What a fascinating giant of a man!"

Ali remembered that Amm Abduh was the only person whom he had not introduced to Samara. "He is a
giant," he said. "But he hardly utters a word. He does
everything, but he rarely speaks. It often seems to us that
he lives in an eternal present, but we cannot be sure. The
most marvelous thing about him is a that any description
you care to give of him proves to be true; he is strong
and weak, there and not there; he is the prayer leader at
the neighboring mosque and a pimp!"

Samara laughed for a long time. "Honestly," she said,
"I adored him at first sight!"

"When will it be our turn!" said Ragab without thinking.

Sana turned her gaze out to the Nile like a fugitive,
and he put his arm apologetically around her. Uncon-
nected questions poured into Anis' head. Had this group
of friends been gathered before as they were tonight—
clad differently—in Roman times? Had they witnessed
the burning of Rome? And why had the moon split off
from the earth, dragging the mountains behind her? And
who was it, in the French Revolution, who had been
killed in his bathroom by a beautiful woman? And how
many of his contemporaries had died—as a result—of
chronic constipation? And how long after the Fall did
Adam have his first quarrel with Eve? Did Eve never try
to blame him for the tragedy brought about by her own
hand?

Layla looked at Samara. "Are you always clear-
headed?" she asked her.

"Coffee and cigarettes—nothing else."

"As for us, if ever we heard of a crackdown on drugs, we'd all be at our wits' end," Mustafa remarked.

"Is it that bad!"

Ragab remembered that they had some whiskey with them. She accepted a glass gladly and he rose to fetch it. Then she asked why they were all so attached to the water pipe. No one volunteered a reply—until Ali said: "It's the focal point of our gatherings. None of us is really happy except when we are here."

She nodded, agreeing that it was a very pleasant party. Then Saniya Kamil addressed her. "You can't escape so easily—you have plenty to say that goes right to the heart of the matter!"

"I don't want to repeat clichés. Nor do I want to come across as a piece of bad didactic theater!"

"But we want to know your opinion!" Ahmad protested.

"I expound it week after week," Samara said, and took a sip of her whiskey. "But what do you have to say about it?" she continued.

"Well," began Mustafa, "for the first half of the day we earn our living, and then afterward we all get into a little boat and float off into the blue."

Now, genuinely interested, she asked, "Are you not concerned at all by what goes on around you?"

"We sometimes find it useful, as material for jokes."

She smiled disbelievingly. Mustafa went on: "Perhaps you are saying to yourself, They are Egyptians, they are Arabs, they are human beings, and in addition they are educated, and so there cannot be a limit to their concerns.

But the truth is that we are not Egyptian or Arab or human; we belong to nothing and no one—except this houseboat . . ."

She laughed, as she might at a good joke. Mustafa continued: "As long as the floats are sound, and the ropes and chains strong, and Amm Abduh is awake, and the pipe filled, then we have no concerns."

"Why!" she exclaimed, and then thought for a minute. "No," she amended. "I will not be tempted into the abyss. I will not allow myself to be a moralizing bore."

"Don't take Mustafa too literally," Ali suggested. "We are not as egotistical as he makes out. But we can see that the ship of state sails on without need of our opinion or support; and that any further thinking on our part is worth nothing, and would very likely bring distress and high blood pressure in its wake."

High blood pressure. Like adulterated kif. The medical student turns hypochondriac the moment he enters college. The Director General himself is no worse than the operating room. That first day in the operating room! Like the first death I knew, the death of those most precious to me. This visitor is interesting even before she opens her mouth. She is beautiful. She smells wonderful. And the night is a lie, since it is the negative of day. And when dawn breaks, tongues will be made dumb. But what is it that you have tried in vain to remember all evening?

Khalid Azzuz turned to Samara. "Your writing shows a literary talent."

"One that has never been tested."

"Doubtless you have a plan."

"I am mad about the theater, first of all."

"What about the cinema?" Ragab asked.

"Oh, my ambitions do not go so far," she replied.

"But the theater is nothing but talk!" he retorted.

Mustafa smiled. "Just like our little society here."

Samara replied earnestly now. "No! The opposite is true: the theater is . . . concentrated; every word has to have a meaning."

"And that is the fundamental difference between the theater and our group," Mustafa suggested.

Suddenly her eyes fell on Anis, who was sending the water pipe around the circle, as if she had discovered him for the first time. "Why don't you speak?" she demanded.

. . . She is tempting you, so that she can say to you, when it comes to it: *I am not a whore.* She reminds me of someone. I cannot remember who. Possibly Cleopatra, or the woman who sells tobacco down in the alley. She's a Scorpio too. Does she not realize that I am absorbed in abstractions of an erotic nature?

Mustafa excused him. "He who works does not speak," he said.

"Why does he do it all himself?"

"It is his favorite pastime," Mustafa replied, "and he allows no one to help him."

"He is the master of ceremonies here," added Ragab. "Sometimes we call him the master of pleasures. Any of us old hands are inexperienced amateurs compared to him, for he manages never to wake up."

"But he must be clearheaded first thing in the morning at least!" Samara protested.

"For a few minutes, during which he bellows for one of his 'magic' cups of coffee, and then . . . !"

Samara addressed her next remarks to Anis. "Tell me yourself," she said. "What do you think about during those moments?"

He did not meet her eyes as he spoke. "I ask myself why I am alive."

"Splendid—and how do you answer that question?"

"Generally," he replied, "I'm high again before I get the chance."

They all laughed, rather too long, and he laughed along with them, his eyes passing over the other women through the billowing clouds of smoke. There was no love in their eyes for the visitor; there was a lion among them, one who devoured the flesh and threw the bones to the others. The new visitor's bones were filled with a disquieting kind of marrow.

But as long as the midge is a mammal, we need not fear. The fact is, were it not for the planets' revolution around the sun, we would soon know immortality at first hand.

Ragab looked at his watch. "Time for us to stop this babbling," he said earnestly. "Tonight has been a milestone in our lives. For the first time, a serious person has graced us with her presence. Someone who has something none of us possesses. Who knows? Perhaps with the passing of time we will find the answer to many questions that have up to now remained unanswered . . ."

She looked at him cautiously. "Are you making fun of me, Ragab?"

"Oh, I wouldn't dream of it! But I do hope that you will become part of our circle here..."

"I hope so too—and I won't miss any opportunity that time allows."

There was an air of defeated resignation as people prepared to leave. The curse that puts an end to everything took hold. Was that the thought which had slipped my mind for so long? There was nothing left in the brazier of the pipe except ash. One by one they left; until he was on his own. Another night dies. From beyond the balcony, the night observed him... and here was Amm Abduh, setting the room to rights.

"Did you see the newcomer?" Anis asked him.

"As much as my old eyes could."

"They say she's a detective!"

"Ah!"

As the old man was on the point of leaving, Anis said to him, "You must go and find a girl for me. A girl to go with this pitch-dark night."

"It's so late at night—there will be no one out in the street now."

"Go on, you great lump!"

"But I've just washed for the dawn prayer!"

"You want to last even longer than you have already, do you? Go on!"

From the ashtray, he took the end of one of the cigarettes she had smoked during the evening. There was just the orange filter left, and part of the white end, squashed. He looked at it for a long time, and then he put it back, in the middle of a little heap of dead midges. The river breathed a watery scent, musky and female. He thought of entertaining himself by counting the stars, but he lacked the will. If there is no one watching our planet and studying our strange habits, then we are lost. How, I wonder, does the observer of our evenings full of laughter interpret what goes on between the meetings and the partings? Perhaps he would say: There are small gatherings that puff out a dust that thickens the atmospheric veil around the planet; and from these groups there come obscure sounds that we will not understand as long as we are without any idea of their composition. The gatherings increase in size from time to time, which means that they must become more numerous through some intrinsic or extrinsic motive. And it is thus not impossible that there is a primitive form of life on that cold planet—contrary to the opinion of some, who hold that it is impossible for life to exist in other than fiery atmospheres. It is extraordinary how these small gatherings disappear, to return repeatedly in this way without any clear goal, a fact that adds weight to the argument against life here—life in the proper sense at least . . .

He hitched his long tunic up over his shins and laughed loudly, so that the watcher would hear and see him. Yes, we do have life, he thought; we have penetrated so deeply in our understanding of it that we have realized that there is no meaning; and you too will penetrate deeper and deeper, and still, no one will be able to predict what will come to be. You will be no more astonished than Julius Caesar was when he was first struck by that immortal beauty tumbling from the rolled-up carpet . . .

"Who is the girl?" the bewildered Caesar asked.

And she replied, utterly confident in her beauty: "Cleopatra, Queen of Egypt."

7 ≈

Anis leaned against the rail of the balcony and gazed at the peaceful sunset. The breeze blew in through the neck of his robe to caress his body. It carried to him, along with the scent of the water and the greenery, the voice of Amm Abduh as he led the prayer in the little mosque near the houseboat. The black coffee was still bitter in his mouth, and his mind was still partly in thrall to the Caliph Ibn Tulun, in whose distant reign he had been wandering for a while before his siesta. He usually dreaded the short time between sipping the coffee and embarking on his evening's journey, in case something happened to bring the mysterious, causeless grief down upon him. But the boat began to rock slightly in time to a faint vibration on the gangway, and he wondered who could be coming so early. Leaving the balcony, he entered the main room just as Samara Bahgat appeared from behind the screen by the door.

She approached him, smiling. He regarded her, astonished. They shook hands. She apologized for coming so early, but he welcomed her in, genuinely pleased. She went out onto the balcony as eagerly as if she were about to see the Nile for the first time, and let her lively, cheerful gaze wander over the sleepy evening scene. She gazed for a long time at the acacia blossoms with their red and violet tints. Then she turned to him and they looked at each other, curiously on her part and with a certain confusion on his. He invited her to sit down, but she went first to the bookshelves to the left of the door, and looked over the titles with interest. Then she took a seat beside his usual place in the middle of the semicircle. He sat down in turn, and said again how pleased he was that she had come early after her weeklong absence. He compared her simple outfit of white blouse and gray skirt with his long white tunic. Perhaps it was because of her work that, unlike other women's, the neck of the blouse did not show her cleavage. Or perhaps because she was a serious girl.

Suddenly she asked: "You were once married, and had a child—is that not so?"

Before he could reply, she apologized, taking back the intrusion with her tone of voice, adding that she believed that Ali al-Sayyid had mentioned it once in the course of telling her about his friends. He replied with a bow of the head. But when he saw the curiosity unsated in her beautiful hazel eyes, he said: "Yes. When I was a student from the countryside, alone in Cairo. Mother and daughter died within the month, from the same illness." Then he added, with a detached simplicity: "That was twenty years ago."

He was reminded of the story of the spider and the fly. He realized, annoyed, that he had hardly started on his journey yet. He was afraid that he would meet with words of pity from her, but she expressed her feelings by a prolonged silence. Then she turned to the bookshelves. "They tell me that you are very keen on history and culture. But, as far as I know, you do not write on those subjects."

He raised the wide eyebrows that suited his broad, pale face in apparent rejection or scorn. She smiled. "So why did you stop studying?" she asked.

"I had no success at it," he replied. "Then I ran out of money, and managed to get a job at the Ministry of Health on the recommendation of one of the doctors who taught me at medical school."

"Perhaps the work doesn't agree with you."

"I can't complain."

He looked at his watch, and then poured a little fluid from a bottle onto the charcoal in the brazier. He put a match to it and placed the brazier in the doorway of the balcony. But now she questioned him again.

"Don't you feel lonely, or . . . ?"

He interrupted her with a laugh. "I don't have time for that."

She laughed in turn. "In any case," she said, "I am happy to have found you in your right mind this time."

"Not entirely," he said. He had seen her looking at the newly lit charcoal, so he pointed, smiling, at the dregs in the bottom of the coffee cup. She accepted the evidence, and began to praise riverside life. He confessed that he himself was relatively new to it. "We gathered in any number of apartments, but the nosy neighbors never once left us in peace!"

And then he laughed, but this time in a different, exultant way. She looked at him inquiringly. He laughed again, and then pointed to his head. "The journey has begun," he said, "and your eyes are beautiful."

"And where is the connection?"

"There is no connection between any one thing and another," he announced, as if it were an axiom.

"Not even between the firing of a bullet and the death of a person?"

"Not even then—for the bullet is a rational invention, but death . . ."

She laughed. "Did you know?" she said, "I came early on purpose so that I could be alone with you."

"Why?"

"Because you are the only one who hardly speaks at all."

The lift of his eyebrows showed that he did not accept this, but she did not retract this time. "Even if you are talking to yourself all the time!"

A silence separated them. He sat looking at the gathering mists, and realized that her early arrival had caused him to miss his usual contemplation of the evening's leisurely entrance. But he was not sorry. They heard the familiar cough from outside. "Amm Abduh," he murmured. She spoke about him with interest, and put a whole string of questions about him to Anis. He answered simply that no, the man was never ill, and that no, the weather did not affect him, and that no, he did not know how old he was, just as he could not imagine him ever dying.

"Would you accept," she asked now, "if I invited you all to the Semiramis Hotel?"

"I think not," he replied uncomfortably. "As for myself, it's impossible." And he assured her that he never left the houseboat except to go to the Archives Department of the Ministry.

"It seems that you don't like me!" she said.

"On the contrary!" he protested. "You're a sweet girl!"

Now the night had drawn in. The boat swayed under many footsteps, and a clamor of voices rose on the gangway. The rocking motion made Samara uneasy. "We live on the water," he told her. "The houseboat always moves like this when people arrive."

The friends appeared one by one from behind the screened door. They were astonished to find Samara there, but welcomed her warmly. Saniya put a special complexion on this early visit, and jestingly congratulated Anis. And shortly after that, his hands were busy as usual, and the water pipe circulated.

Ragab poured Samara a whiskey. Anis saw Sana snatching a furtive look at Samara from beneath her curls, and he smiled. As the coals glowed, he became merry. He offered the water pipe to Samara, but she declined, and all his encouragement was in vain. Everything was silent, save for the bubbling of the pipe. Then they were swept away on a stream of diverse remarks. American planes had made strikes on North Vietnam. Like the Cuban crisis, remember? And as for the rumors, there was no end to them. The world was teetering on the brink of an abyss. The price of meat, the problems of the government food cooperatives—and what about the workers and the peasants? And corruption, and hard currency, and socialism, and the way the streets were jammed with private cars? And Anis said to himself: All these things lie in the bowl of the pipe, to go up in smoke, like the vegetable dish, *mulukhiya*, which Amm Abduh cooked for lunch that day. Like our old motto, "If I were not, I would wish to be." And when a light like the light of these embers blazes in the heavens, the astronomer says that a star has exploded, and in turn the planets around it, and everything has been blown to dust. And one day the dust fell onto the surface of the earth and life sprang from it . . . And after all that, they tell me: "I will cut two days from your salary!" Or they tell me: "I am not a whore!" The poet al-Ma'arri summed it up in one line—a line which I cannot remember, which I do not care if I remember or not. Al-Ma'arri was blind, and could not have seen Samara when she lived in his time.

"My husband is trying to get a reconciliation."

"God forbid!"

Blind, and could not see. The thread was cut, and some splendid thing was scattered away. The important thing is that we preserve . . . preserve what? Tomorrow we have a wearisome task; tomorrow is the day of the annual accounts. In the prison house of the Archives Department. A museum for insects. Midges, of course, being mammals . . .

"But you are a beautiful blonde," Samara was saying to Layla. "Really you are."

Khalid Azzuz spoke, and it was clear that he meant Layla. "Her real problem," he began, "is the problem of the country as a whole; that is, she's a modern girl—but the husband is bourgeois!"

Anis looked out at the night. He saw the lamps of the opposite shore, slipping into the river's depths like pillars of light. And from a houseboat out of sight, carried on the breeze, came the sound of singing and music. Perhaps a wedding party. As Muhammad al-Arabi had sung on the night of your wedding: "Look! What a wonder. I fell for a peasant girl!" And my uncle had said: "God preserve you, and let your house be full of fine children, but be careful, there are only two acres left . . ." How beautiful the village was, with the garden smelling of orange blossom; a perfume as heady as musk behind the ears of fine women . . .

"What a suggestion!" someone was exclaiming.

"But it's a wonderful idea!" Samara replied eagerly. "And this way we will really get to know each other; there's no room for pretenses!"

"But what do you mean by it?"

"I mean the primary concern of your lives!"

"Sounds like a probe to me!"

"If you have any doubts about me at all, then I should leave this minute!" Samara protested.

"Let's start with you, then," Ahmad said cautiously. "Tell us about your primary concern."

She appeared not to be surprised by the question, and said simply, in a way that seemed very candid: "Mine, at the moment, is that I try my hand at writing a play."

"Plays are not written without a reason!" Mustafa said maliciously.

She took a leisurely puff at her cigarette, narrowing her eyes in thought, hesitating. Ali's smile betrayed his sympathy for her, and he said, to encourage her: "The atmosphere here is clearly not conducive to anything except cynicism and triviality. I think you have a strong character, though—and you should stand firm!"

She lowered her eyes, as if she were contemplating the coals in the brazier. "So be it," she said. "The truth is that I believe in being serious."

There was a barrage of questions. Serious? Serious about everything? Could we not seriously believe in absurdity? And seriousness, moreover, implies that life has a meaning—but what is this meaning? Finally Ragab cried, "You have a sorceress here before you! With one stroke of her pen she will turn farce into political theater!" He turned to Samara. "But do you really believe in that?"

"I hope so."

"Speak frankly. Tell me how you can. We would welcome this miracle of belief with all our hearts!"

They discussed the higher basis on which life's meaning had formerly rested. They agreed that this basis had now gone forever. What new foundation could there possibly be? Samara summed it up: "The will to live!"

They exchanged their thoughts. The will to live was something sure and solid, but it could lead to absurdity. Indeed, what was to stop it? Was the will to live alone sufficient to create heroes? For the hero was someone who sacrificed his will to live in the service of some other thing, loftier in his eyes than life; how, according to her theory, could that higher glory ever be reached?

Samara spoke again. "I mean that in our search we should turn toward the will to live itself, not any one foundation in which it is impossible to believe. The will to live is what makes us cleave to real life at times when, if it were left to our intellects alone, we would commit suicide. This will itself is the sure foundation granted to us, so that by it we might rise above ourselves . . ."

Mustafa spoke. "You've turned Marx upside down," he said. "Not 'from above to below,' but 'from below to above'!"

"There is no philosophy there," she protested. "But this is my primary concern. Now it's your turn."

Curses on you all. There is no worse an enemy to the water pipe's pleasures than thinking. Twenty pipes, and all for nothing, or nearly nothing. A date palm seems to be the firmest believer of all. The perseverance of the midges is also worthy of admiration. But if the plaints of Omar Khayyam lose their ardor, then say goodbye to ease. All these mockers and scoffers are merely complex atomic formations. And each of these individuals is breaking down into a certain number of atoms. Losing their form and color . . . changing entirely . . . until there is nothing left of them that can be seen with the naked eye . . . until there is nothing there except voices.

The voice, then, of Ragab al-Qadi: "My primary concern is art."

And the voice of Mustafa Rashid: "Actually, his primary concern is love—or, to be more exact, women."

Samara's voice, doubtful: "Is that really what concerns you?"

"No more and no less."

Her voice had prompted Ali's voice to reply. He said: "My primary concern is artistic criticism!"

The mocking voice of Mustafa: "Nonsense; his real concern is to dream—dreaming itself, that is, regardless of the contents of the dream. Criticism? He criticizes simply to flatter friends or destroy enemies—and to squeeze a certain amount of money out of it as well!"

"But then how can he want the dream to come true?"

"That does not matter to him at all. But when the pipe is generous in its bliss, he scratches his formidable nose and says: 'Contemplate, my children, the distance man has traveled, from the caves to outer space! Bastards all, you will soon sport among the stars like gods.'"

The inquiry turned to Ahmad. His voice spoke hesitantly. "My first concern is . . . to keep up my reputation."

Mustafa's voice, interrupting again: "This man is in a different situation altogether. He's a Muslim, to begin with; he prays and fasts, and he is a model husband whose attitude toward the women here is one of complete indifference. Perhaps his primary concern is that his daughter gets married!"

Khalid's voice: "He is the only one of us who will live after death."

Anis became tired of his clamorous solitude and called Amm Abduh to change the water in the pipe. The man seemed, while he was present, to be the only thing existing in this vocal wilderness. One voice said that his concern was to remember; and another that it was to forget. And Anis himself wondered why the Tartar hordes had stopped on the border . . .

"I have no concerns!" cried Layla's voice.

To which the voice of Khalid replied: "Or rather, I am her first concern!"

Saniya's voice said: "Mine is that my husband divorces me—and that Ali divorces both his wives . . ."

Samara's voice tried to draw out Sana's voice, but it did not utter a word. Ragab's voice said: "Tell me your primary concern!"

And Sana's voice said: "No"; but the voice of a kiss whispered, indistinct and blurred. As for the voice of Khalid, it said: "My first concern is . . . anarchy!"

Laughter rang out. Then a silence reigned, like an interval for rest, and the void had complete dominion.

Amm Abduh approached. "A woman has just fallen from the eighth floor of the Suya Company building," he said.

Anis regarded him anxiously. "How did you find out?"

"I hurried over when I heard the scream. It was a shocking sight."

Ali's voice: "Luckily we're far from the street—we can't hear anything."

"Did the woman commit suicide or was she murdered?"

"God only knows," replied the old man. Then he hurried out to the street.

Ali suggested going out to see what was going on, but this was rejected by the company. The shock of the news had returned the atoms to their original formation, and people were themselves again. Anis was glad that he had escaped from his wearisome solitude. The company of madmen was better than being alone. It was Mustafa's turn to speak now, but Ali wanted to avenge himself first.

"He's a lawyer," Ali began, "who lost some of his best clients when the constituencies were reorganized, and who lives now off the misdeeds of ordinary people. His first concern, after getting an advance on his fees, is the Absolute; and this even though he is ruthless when it comes to getting the balance of the fees!"

"So you're devout!" said Samara.

"God forbid!"

"But what is the Absolute?"

It was Ali who replied. "Sometimes he looks at the sky, and sometimes he retreats into his shell—and sometimes he is sure that he is close to it, but there are no words to describe it. Khalid has advised him to go to a gland specialist."

"But he is one of the serious people at any rate?"

"Not at all. His Absolute is absurd."

"Could you describe him as a philosopher?"

"In the modern sense of philosophy, if you wished; that is, the philosophy that combines theft and imprisonment and sexual perversion à la Jean Genet."

Anis recalled his last meeting with Nero. No, he was not the monster people said he was. He had said that when he found that he was emperor he killed his mother; and then when he became a god, he burned Rome to the ground. Before all that, he was just an ordinary human being—one who loved art. And this was why he now enjoyed the bliss of paradise. Anis laughed aloud—to find all eyes turned upon him, and Samara addressing him. "Your turn now, master of ceremonies; what is the most important thing for you?"

Anis answered without a second thought. "To be your lover," he said.

Everybody roared with laughter—and Ragab burst out: "But . . ." before remembering himself. Everyone laughed all the more, and in spite of the embarrassment, Samara persisted in getting a reply. Ahmad answered for him. "To kill the Director General."

Samara laughed. "At last I have found somebody serious," she said.

"But he only thinks about that when he is clear-headed."

"Even so!"

Amm Abduh returned. He stood by the screen in front of the door. "The woman committed suicide," he said. "After a quarrel with her lover."

There was a short silence, broken by Khalid. "She did the right thing," he said. "Change the water in the pipe, Amm Abduh."

"So there is still love after all," murmured Samara.

Khalid spoke again. "The woman most likely killed herself when she was serious. We, on the other hand, will not."

Ahmad said that every living creature was serious, and built its life upon that foundation; and that absurdity did not usually occur to the mind. One might find a killer without a motive in a novel such as *L'Etranger,* but in real life? Beckett himself was the first to take swift legal action against any publisher who broke the contract on his absurdist works!

Samara was not convinced. She maintained that what was in the mind must somehow influence behavior—or, at the very least, feelings. Take, for example, the nihilism everywhere, the immorality, the spiritual suicides! But human beings are still human beings, and they must rebel against it, even if only once a year! . . .

Ragab suggested that she stay until dawn, to watch the sun come up over the acacias.

She declined the invitation, and at midnight took her leave. When they suggested one of them drive her home, she thanked them but refused.

After she had gone, there was a silence like that of rest after toil. Fatigue threatened to overtake them all. Anis decided to tell them about his atomic experiment, but he was forced by his own lassitude to abandon the idea.

"What is behind this strange and fascinating woman?" Ahmad wondered aloud.

Ali's large eyes were red now, and his great nose looked almost bulbous. "She wants to know everything," he said. "And she wants to make a friend of everyone worthy of friendship."

"Could she possibly be thinking that she might win us over one day?" asked Mustafa. And Khalid added: "In that case, we should try to win her over into one of these three bedrooms."

"That's Ragab's task!"

Sana went pale; but no value was attached to any comment now, after so many pipes.

"We must find a successor for Sana," Khalid said next. The girl gave Ragab a hard look, and he humored her: "People say anything when they're high..." Khalid, however, would not let it drop. "Is it easy for a trivial man to love a serious woman, do you think?"

The water pipe went round, and eyelids drooped. They took the brazier out to the balcony and blew the ash off the coals, which glowed and spat sparks. Anis went toward the door to the balcony to feel the damp night breeze. He gazed in wonderment at the fire, surrendering to its enchantment. He thought: Nobody knows the secret of power like the Delta does. Geckos and rats and midges, and the river water; all these are my family, but only the Delta knows the secret of power. The North was an enchanted world, covered with forests that knew no day except spots of light glancing in through the lattice of leaves and branches. And one day the clouds fled away, and an unwelcome guest with cracked skin and gray face appeared, whose name was Drought. What can we do, when Death is at our heels? The green shriveled away, and the birds migrated, and the animals perished. I said: Death is coming, creeping nearer, stretching out his hand. My cousins, they went southward in search of the easy life, and fruit off the tree, even if it was at the end of the earth. But my family had made for the standing lakes of Nile water, and we had no weapons save resolution, and no witness to our mad, brave deeds except the Delta. And waiting for us there, the thorny plants and reptiles

and wild beasts and flies and gnats, and there was a savage
feast of Death; and no witness save the Delta. They said:
All we can do is fight, inch by inch, welter in blood and
sweat. Forearms bloody. Eyes staring and ears pricked,
and not a thing to hear except the advance of Death. And
the ghosts were everywhere, the vultures wheeling, waiting for victims. No time save for action, no armistice for
burying our dead. No one there to ask: Where are they
going? Wonders were worked, the seeds of miracles were
sown, and no witness save the Delta . . .

8 ❧

When a new evening begins, the feeling of immanence intensifies. All existence is at peace. The thought of the end is far away, and there is a rare chance to give rein to notions of eternity. Because the sky is moonlit, the neon light has been put out, and we content ourselves with a dim blue lamp hung over the door to the balcony. The faces of my companions look pale. Out beyond the balcony, the moon—which is too high to be seen from here—casts a silvery rhombus over the semicircle of smokers.

"You've read Samara's article about the new film, of course."

"You mean about Ragab al-Qadi!" someone interjected.

Of course, he has not. He does not read newspapers or magazines. Like Louis XVI, he knows nothing of what goes on in the world.

Layla said, out of regard for Sana's feelings: "Seriousness! Indeed! I never paid much attention to that—I knew from the beginning that she had come with another aim in mind."

"Let's dance," Sana said to Ragab.

"There's no music," he replied, with odious placidity.

"Think how much we've danced without music!"

"Be patient, my dear—or the pipe will never get going."

He thinks that he is the center of the universe, and that the pipe only circulates because of him. But really the pipe goes around for the same reason that anything does; if the planets traveled in a straight line, then the order of nature would be altered. Last night I believed totally in eternal life—but on my way to the office I forgot the reason why.

"I thought that the article smacked of 'commitment,'" Khalid said sardonically. "What did you think, Ragab?"

Ragab replied, as if Sana was not there: "I thought it was a compliment, an approach, on her part."

"But what is certain is that she has deserted us for days!"

That hidden quarter-moon floods the darkness with an intoxicated glow, like the sleepy eye of a violet. Do you remember how weary the moon became, staying miraculously full through all the nights of battle in the first days of Islam? Here is the warrior once more, leaping into a new fray; and like all warriors', his costume has the hardness of chain mail . . .

Ragab said, with even more callous indifference to his companion: "I called Samara to thank her, and said that I would like to visit her were I not afraid of embarrassing her—and she said, amazed, that there was no question of embarrassment!"

"An open invitation!"

"So just a few minutes later I was knocking on her

door—and whom did I find inside but our friend Ali al-Sayyid!"

The "friend" was subjected to a hail of abuse.

"I thanked her and drank some coffee, and said that her article had all but made a new man of me!"

"Hypocrite, son of hypocrites, descended from a long line of bred-in-the-bone hypocrites," Ali intoned.

"My gaze was drawn irresistibly to her allure—while from her vocal cords issued the sort of honeyed tones that take a lot of effort to get past the censors!"

"Deluded fantasy," said Ali. "It was a normal conversation—conducted in a normal voice."

"But you were engrossed in a heated discussion with a film director, on the point of clinching a deal—"

Ali laughed loudly. "That was about a case of whiskey, nothing else. Which will shortly be consumed by the people on this infernal houseboat."

"And was it confined to honeyed tones?" asked Mustafa Rashid.

"What more can you expect from an almost formal occasion? But even so, the serious miss was swathed in a veil of femininity, like a butterfly flitting from flower to flower—or Amm Abduh doing the rounds of his street girls!"

Sana's voice sounded like the top string of a zither when the player strikes it by accident. "What a magician you are," she said.

He smiled at her—a faint smile, which in the pallid blue light looked like a grimace. "My dear little thing," he said.

"I'm not little, if you don't mind!" she snapped.

"Little in years, but how great in . . . in stature—"

"Oh, spare me clichés that were old in the days of the Mameluke sultans!"

Ali sighed. "Oh to be in the Mameluke age—as long as we could be sultans, of course."

Sana replied, with undisguised dislike: "And oh how quickly the people on this boat turn into heartless beasts!"

But beasts do have hearts. And they are only savage when faced by enemies. I will not forget the whale as it retreated from the boat, telling me: *I am the whale who saved Jonah.* How many millions and millions of eyes have gazed at the Nile lying still in the moonlight. No better sign of Samara's sincerity than the passage of migrating birds. And as for poor Sana, she has forgotten about the cave dwellers in the age of her first youth . . .

"This tobacco!" Anis cried. "It's burning like paper!" And he wrapped it in a handkerchief to squeeze it down, all the while taking part in the Japan Olympics, running races and lifting weights and setting new world records. Then the telephone rang.

Ragab rose to answer it as if he was expecting a call. Anis could not hear what he was saying, apart from isolated phrases such as "Of course" and "Right away." He replaced the receiver and turned to the company. "If you will excuse me," he said; and turning to Sana: "I might be back at the end of the evening." And with that, he left. The houseboat shook under his powerful tread.

Sana twitched. It seemed to the others that she was almost in tears. Nobody said a word. Everyone looked questioningly—but Ali shook his head.

At last Mustafa addressed Sana, speaking to her

gently. "Don't. The romantic era is long gone. It's the age of realism now."

And Layla said, concealing a gloating smile: "It is an accepted rule here—nothing is worth regretting..."

"Hang romanticism! And regrets!" cried Sana vehemently.

"He has gone to meet a producer, I assure you," said Ali. "But you really should bear in mind that your friend is a professional ladies' man!"

Ahmad stood up. "I'll bring you a whiskey," he said. "But do try to pull yourself together."

Then Saniya spoke. She was startlingly blunt. "And if worse comes to worst," she said, "you've still got Ahmad and Mustafa!"

"And what about me, you bastards!" shouted Anis wildly; and then he added roughly, spitting the words out: "Dissipated, addicted wretches!"

Everyone convulsed with laughter. "Do you think he's really gone to see Samara?" Mustafa wondered.

"No, no, no," said Ali.

"It wouldn't be unusual for him to be after a woman!"

"Would somebody please tell me," asked Layla, "why on earth she came here if it wasn't because of him?"

"Nothing's impossible, I admit," said Ali. "But Samara is not a naïve young girl. I don't think she would be satisfied with being a nine-day wonder."

"What is it that makes some men so incredibly presumptuous?" Mustafa wondered.

"Well, any star in his position is bound to have a certain charisma."

"It isn't just the aura of a star, or even elegance and good looks; he is simply sexuality itself!"

"Oh, let the women speak about that," said Ahmad. But Ali went on: "Women fall in love, but they don't say why!"

"In that case," advised Khalid, "consult your pituitary gland."

Sana took a mattress and went out onto the balcony to sit on her own. "Is she the feminine ideal you are searching for?" Ali asked Mustafa, surreptitiously indicating Sana. Mustafa tersely replied that she was not.

"The permissive society!" said Khalid. "Free love! It's the only remedy for all these ills."

"Damn you all," Anis said suddenly. "It is you who are responsible for the decline of Roman civilization."

Everyone roared. "You're unusually touchy tonight!" Ahmad observed of him.

"This filthy tobacco."

"But it is often like that."

"What about the moon?" Anis asked. "Do you know what part it plays in the comedy?"

"What comedy?"

"The comedy of comedies!"

The water pipe circulated without ceasing. They were silent, to collect their scattered thoughts. There were no more accusations to make. History? The future? It was all nothing. Neither more nor less. Zero. Miracle of miracles. The unknown was revealed in the moonlight. Amm Abduh's voice came from outside, as he chanted words that no one could make out. Somebody laughed; and somebody else said that it was amazing how quickly the time had passed. They could hear the waves lapping against the bottom of the boat. Yes indeed, the part played by the moon in all this . . . And the part played by the ox, blindfolded at the waterwheel. One day the sheikh said to me: "You love aggression, and God does not love aggressors," as the blood poured from my nose. Or perhaps the sheikh had said that to the other man, and perhaps the blood had been pouring from his nose. How can you trust in anything after that? And then the same voice said: "Amazing how quickly the time has passed."

Ahmad sighed. "Time to go," he said.

That is the death knell of our evenings. An indolent activity spread among them, and then Ahmad and Mustafa left, followed by Khalid and Layla. Ali and Saniya, however, slipped into the bedroom overlooking the garden. Amm Abduh came to tidy up the room, and Anis complained to him about the quality of the tobacco. The old man replied that there was nothing except bad tobacco on the market.

A sneeze came from the balcony. Anis suddenly remembered Sana. He crawled out to the balcony on all fours. Then he leaned against the rail, stretching his legs out in front of him. "Beautiful evening," he murmured. The moonlight had retreated from the balcony to the other side of the boat, toward the road, drawing its glittering carpet behind it.

"Do you think he will come back?" she asked.

"Who?"

"Ragab!"

"How miserable it is, to be asked a question one cannot answer!"

"He said that he might come back at the end of the evening."

"Might."

"Am I annoying you?"

"Of course not!"

"Do you think I should wait?"

Anis gave a light laugh. "People have been waiting for their saviors for a thousand years."

"Are you laughing at me, like them?"

"Nobody is laughing at you. It's just their way of talking."

"In any case, you're the nicest."

"Me!"

"You don't say evil things."

"That is because I am dumb."

"And we have something in common."

"What is that?"

"Loneliness."

"You're never alone when you smoke."

"Why don't you flirt with me a bit?"

"The real smoker is self-sufficient."

"How about a little trip on the river in a sailing boat?"

"My legs can hardly carry me."

She sighed. "There's nothing for it. I shall have to leave. There is no one to take me down to the square."

"Amm Abduh will take anyone who has no one to go with."

In the breeze, the moist breaths of the night; and from

behind the locked door of the bedroom, chuckles of laughter. The sky was completely clear, studded with thousands of stars. In the middle of the sky he saw a smiling face, the features obliterated. He began to feel as he had only ever felt when he set the world record at the Olympics. The time had gone so amazingly fast that the true tragedy of the battle appeared now before his eyes. The Persian King Cambyses sat on the dais, his victorious army behind him. On his right, his conquering generals; on his left the Pharaoh, sitting bowed in defeat. The prisoners of war from the Egyptian army were passing before the victorious Cambyses when suddenly the Pharaoh burst into tears. Cambyses turned toward him, asking what it was that made him weep. The Pharaoh pointed to a man walking, head bent, among the captives.

"That man!" he said. "I knew him so long in his glory, it pains me to see him bound in chains!"

9 ⤫

Everything has been prepared for the evening, and now Amm Abduh is giving the call to the sunset prayer. But there is a heavy trial ahead, of waiting; waiting for the enchanted cup of coffee to work its magic. Waiting is a tense feeling of sleeplessness, and there is no cure for it except the balm of eternity. Until then the Nile will not ease you, nor the flocks of white doves; and with an anxious eye you picture your companions of the evening disperse as you picture all endings. The moon, appearing over the acacias, only serves to reinforce this melancholy instead of soothing it away; and as long as that is so, even good actions are succeeded by regret, and the heart is oppressed by any wisdom save that which sounds the death of all wisdoms. Let pains retreat before the magic, never to return. When we emigrate to the moon, we will be the first settlers ever to run from Nothingness to Nothingness. Pity the web of the spider who sang one evening in the village, in time to the croaking frogs. Just before sleeping this afternoon you heard Napoleon, accusing the English of killing him by slow poison. But the English are not the only ones who kill by slow poison . . .

Anis began to pace back and forth between the balcony and the screen by the door. He lit the blue lamp;

and it was then that he felt the fingertips of mercy begin to soothe him inside.

The houseboat shook; voices were raised, heralding life. The company assembled, and the water pipe circulated beneath the eye of the moon.

For the first time, Sana was not there. When Ahmad remarked upon it, comments were quick to follow. "The thing is," said Saniya, "that you are all men in a state of zero gravity—you've lost your bearings."

Ragab appeared unconcerned, occupied as he was with the kif just then.

"You were cruel to her," Ahmad told him. "You didn't think how young she is."

"I can't be a lover and a nanny at the same time."

"But she is only a girl!"

"As I said, I'm not the first artist in her life."

Ahmad said that she had probably been truly in love with him. "If love manages to stay alive for a month in this space age," retorted Ragab, "it can be counted as middle-aged!" And he told them how she had tempted him with her wiles, and how he had refused "like Joseph with Potiphar's wife!" And how love had been responsible for the fabrication of stories since the beginning of time . . . The moonlight shone down on them. Before long it would disappear from view. As Anis stared at his friends, new features were revealed; it was as if he were seeing them for the first time. For he saw them usually with his ears, or through a cloud of smoke, or through their ideas, the way they behaved. But when he focused on their faces spontaneously, penetratingly, he found himself to be a stranger among strangers. He saw ruin in the light wrinkles around Layla's eyes. He glimpsed an icy cruelty in Ragab's mocking smile. The world also appeared strange; he no longer knew where they were in Time; perhaps it did not exist at all. He became aware of the name Samara on their lips—and almost immediately he heard her voice as she joked with Amm Abduh outside. The boat's shaking ran like a shudder through his body. And then she appeared, in a white tailored jacket and skirt, waving her hand in greeting and taking her place on the mattress that was free—Sana's place. She lit a cigarette in a relaxed manner, and no one could detect anything in her bearing to justify Ragab's mysterious behavior the previous night. Innocently, she asked: "Where's Sana?"

Mustafa answered: "In Amm Abduh's hut."

Samara's innocent expression did not change. Mustafa said that perhaps she was looking for the Absolute in there. Samara replied that she ought to look for that in him, not in Amm Abduh's hut. Mustafa continued his mockery. "The fact is, Sana found that Ragab's love was a somewhat impermanent attribute, so she departed in search of something true and unchangeable."

"There's something truly unchangeable in Amm Abduh's hut," Samara rejoined sadly. "Emptiness."

It was true. The old man possessed only the robe he stood in, and he slept on an old couch with no coverlet. That was how Anis had found him when he had moved to the houseboat. He must get him a blanket before winter came.

Mustafa again urged Samara to try the water pipe, and Ragab backed him up. "Why are you so adamant!" he said.

She laughed. "Why do you love it so much? That's the important question!"

"No—it is your abstinence that needs to be explained!"

It was clear to everyone that she had a passionate desire to get to the bottom of this. Very well, then. Why did people adore the pipe's oblivion? Why did they yearn for that stupefied drowsiness?

"Why don't you look up 'addiction' in the Encyclopaedia Britannica," suggested Khalid, but Mustafa added quickly: "Beware of clichés, miss!" She smiled uncertainly as he continued: "And of fatuous words like 'escape' and so on . . ."

"I want to know," she said simply.

"Is this a new investigation?" Ragab asked.

"I will not allow you to keep accusing me like this!"

"Platitudes are worth nothing," challenged Mustafa. "We are all working people—the director of an accounts department, an art critic, an actor, an author, a lawyer, a civil servant. We give to society all that it requires and more. What are we escaping from?"

Her reply was candid. "You are constructing arguments and then knocking them down. I'm simply asking what the water pipe does for you."

Ali al-Sayyid spoke. "As the poet of old said:

> *"Eyes sleepless, eyes sleeping*
> *For some reason or none*

Cast off care if you can,
For care to madness leads . . ."

"So it's because of your cares!" she said, with something resembling triumph.

But Mustafa persisted: "We give our daily concerns our closest attention. We are not good-for-nothings. We are the fathers of families! We have jobs to do!"

As the discussion proceeds, the world seems more and more bizarre. Cares and lazy people and clichés. The drugged debate with reddened eyes. The moon has completely disappeared, but the surface of the water glitters as if it were an unfamiliar, smiling, happy face. What does the woman want? What do the smokers want? They say leisure, and she says addiction. It is extraordinary that the boat does not shake with this debate, but only rocks now under footsteps on the gangway. Amm Abduh came, and took the pipe away to change the water. He brought it back and left again. Anis looked at the glitter of the Nile and smiled. He became aware of Samara's voice calling him—and looked over at her, his hands still busy with the water pipe.

"I would like to hear *your* opinion," she said.

"Miss," he said simply, "get married."

Everybody laughed. "She prefers the role of preacher," said Ragab.

But she was determined not to be embarrassed, and continued with her eyes to urge Anis to speak. But he looked away from her, down at his work. Why do one and one make two?

An annoying woman. Bursting in on us with life's

banalities. What does she want? And how can we ever get high with this battle raging all the time!

When she despaired of him, she turned to Mustafa. "I accept that you take your problems seriously in your daily lives—but what about public life?"

"Do you mean national politics?"

"*And* foreign policy!" she replied.

"And international affairs as well, why not!" said Khalid sarcastically.

She smiled. "And that as well."

"And we must not neglect the politics of the universe either," added Mustafa.

"I see that there are more problems than we imagined!" she said, laughing.

"Now we begin to understand each other," Mustafa went on. "You regret the time we waste in evenings like this one. You consider that it is an escape from our real responsibilities. That were it not for this, we would come up with solutions for the problems of the Arab world and the planet as a whole and the universe as well . . ."

They laughed again. They told Anis that he was the real reason for the sufferings of the world, for the unsolved mysteries of the universe. Mustafa suggested that they throw the water pipe into the Nile, and then divide the work among them. Khalid would concern himself with national policy, and Ali with international affairs, and Mustafa himself with solving the more cosmic difficulties. How would they start? How would they organize themselves? How would they realize socialist ideals on a national democratic basis, without betraying these ideals or oppressing the people? How, after that, would they find a cure for world problems like war and racial discrimination? As for Mustafa, they had to decide whether he would begin by studying science and philosophy or whether he would content himself with meditation, waiting for the ray of light! They also gave careful attention to the challenging obstacles that lay in their path, the dangers awaiting them. Confiscation of personal assets. Imprisonment. Execution . . .

And then someone complained: "Amazing, how quickly the time has passed . . .

The moon had disappeared completely, and on the water there remained only a small scrap of the glittering carpet of light. The water pipe had not ceased in its rounds, and neither had Samara stopped laughing.

Thoughts clashed in Anis' head. Thoughts of the first battles of Islam, of the Crusades, of the courts of the Inquisition. The deaths of great lovers and philosophers, the bloody conflicts between Catholics and Protestants, the age of the early Christian martyrs. The founding fathers' voyage to America, the death of Adila and Haniya, his dealings with the street girls; and the whale that had saved Jonah, and Amm Abduh's job, divided as it was between prayer leading and pimping. The silence of the last watch of the night, which he could never describe; and the fleeting, phosphorescent thoughts that glowed for an instant before vanishing forever.

He became aware of Samara's voice; she was asking everyone what they were like in their youth, at the beginning of their lives.

They laughed. Why do they laugh? It is as if their lives had no beginning. Just distant, Stone Age memories. The village, and then the single room and resolution; resolution in the village and the single room. When the moon rose and set without signaling the end of anything.

"When I was a boy," said Khalid, "there was no question without an answer. The world did not go around, and hope stretched out into the future for a hundred million light years."

Ali said: "I remember wondering once why our fear of death hindered our eternal happiness."

"And one day," added Mustafa, "Anis and I nearly died in a revolutionary demonstration!"

None of this surprised Samara. She began to talk about the possibility of recalling this same ardor, but in a more contemporary form. The others, however, began to discuss the natural treachery of women, how it banished trust in any one of them . . . She said to Mustafa, who was arguing the most strongly: "You are taking refuge from responsibility in the Absolute."

"Responsibility is the way many people take refuge from the Absolute," he replied cynically.

Chicken and egg. As for me, I stack the coals and fill the pipe and light the fire and send the pipe around; and so I get my fill, willy-nilly, of all their rubbish, and the women laugh and dream of love; and time goes by with amazing speed. And each time the cultured young miss wishes to leave, the magician insists on her staying. In a little while, destruction will befall the gathering. Omar

Khayyam, who gave his name to a school of philosophy, now has a hotel called after him where all kinds of fun take place. He told me at our last meeting that if he had lived until now, he would have joined one of the sporting clubs . . .

"Time to go home!"

The men and women left—all except Ragab and Samara.

One thing is sure. They do not know that it is the Nile which has condemned us to ourselves. And that nothing remains of our ancient worship except the cult of the bull god, Apis. And that the real malady is fear of life, not death. And now you will hear the oft-repeated conversation, proceeding in time-honored fashion:

"Would it not be better, my dear, if we took pleasure in love?"

"A nice idea!"

"So . . . ?"

"I told you, *my* dear, that I am serious!"

"Bourgeois mentality, I think."

"Serious, s-e-r-i-o-u-s."

"Then how on earth will you ever give of yourself?"

And when she did not reply he continued: "Only in marriage, for example?"

"Say, real love."

"So come, then . . ."

"Are *you* serious?" she asked.

"I never joke," he replied.

"What about Sana?"

"You know nothing about the mad psychology of puberty."

"I do know some things, you know."

"Would you surrender to me if I promised to be serious too?"

"You are quite charming!"

Now he is bringing his face closer to hers. The old scene will be repeated. And now he is putting his lips to hers. She did not resist, but neither did she respond. He gave her a cold and mocking stare. The knight's ardor waned, and he retreated. The ancient Persian occupation failed this way. Through the passive resistance, that is, of the Pharaonic Egyptians.

Ragab smiled. "Let's stroll in the garden, then," he said.

"But it's so late . . ."

"There's no such thing as time on this houseboat."

The room was empty now. No, it was not empty; there was still the debris of the evening there, and the library and the screen and the refrigerator and the telephone and the neon light and the blue lamp, and two armchairs and the sky-blue carpet with a pink pattern; and also the recumbent figure of an atom-age man. As for those two, they are strolling in the garden, and the dewy grass will cool their heat, and their whispers will linger in the leaves of violet and jasmine. And they could well be dancing, now, to the song of the crickets.

Amm Abduh came to perform his final task. Anis watched him for a while, and then said: "If you found a girl . . ."

"Oh!"

"Before or after washing for the prayer. If you don't, woe betide you."

"One of the men who prayed every dawn prayer with us has died. A good man."

"God spare you. I think you will probably bury us all."

The old man laughed as he took away the brass tray.

Anis' eyes fell on a large white handbag on the mattress where Samara had been sitting. It seemed to him that the bag had a personality; that by some cunning sorcery it was influencing him . . . yes, he was aware of a violent urge to commit a dreadful deed. He stretched out his hand to the bag and opened it.

He saw all the things one would expect, but they seemed to scream of unfamiliarity. He was overwhelmed by the odor of purity. A handkerchief, a small navy-blue bottle, a comb with a silver handle. And a purse, and a pocket notebook. He opened the purse. There were several bank notes in it. He decided to take fifty piasters to give to the girl Amm Abduh would bring—what a delightful idea. Then another, matchless notion occurred, one uniquely capable of stirring up all kinds of mischief: he took the notebook and slid it into his pocket. Then he closed the bag, and began to shake with laughter.

He would do a little surgery again. The operation he had failed at so many years ago. Open up a heart that was closed to him. His youth would be renewed. His prime would come again. The girl would say everything which occurred to the mind and everything which did not. And then she would wonder how one primeval protozoan could contain all these wonders. And she would ask me when it was that I was a volcano before the layers of dead ash settled over me. And I do not know the answer...

I do not know the answer, but perhaps you do, you on whose memory history was built. He sat in front of me like a statue and I said: "Are you in truth the Pharaoh? Are you Thutmose III?"

He answered, in a voice that reminded me of Mustafa Rashid: "Yes."

"What are you doing?"

"I am sharing the throne with my sister Hatshepsut."

Earnestly I said: "Many people ask why you languish in her shadow."

"She is the Queen."

"But you are also the King."

"She is powerful, and she wishes to have dominion over everything."

"But you are the greatest general of Egypt, and the most mighty judge..."

"But I have not yet leaped into battle, or passed judgment!"

"I am telling you what you will become. Do you not understand?"

"And how do you know that?"

"From history. Everyone knows that."

He appeared to my eyes. He was looking at me with

the expression people reserve for idiots. I persisted. "It is history. Believe me."

"But you are speaking of a future which is unknown."

And I said, like someone who is speaking in a nightmare, helplessly: "It is history! Believe me!"

10 ❧

The major theme of the drama is the Serious versus the Absurd.

Absurdity is the loss of meaning, the meaning of anything. The collapse of belief—belief in anything. It is a passage through life propelled by necessity alone, without conviction, without real hope. This is reflected in the character in the form of dissipation and nihilism, and heroism is transformed into mockery and myth. Good and evil are equal; and one is adopted over the other— if adopted at all—with the simple motive of egotism, or cowardice, or opportunism. All values perish, and civilization comes to an end.

What must be studied in this context is the problem of religious people who take the path of the absurd. They are not lacking in faith, but still, in a practical sense, they lead futile lives. How can this be explained? Have they misunderstood the nature of religion? Or is it their faith which is unreal, which is a matter of routine—a rootless faith, which serves merely as a cover for the most vile kinds of opportunism and exploitation? This point demands closer study, as does the question of whether I should deal with it in the play or treat it as an independent issue.

As for seriousness, it means belief. But belief in what? It is not enough for us to know what we must believe in. It is also necessary that our belief has the sincerity of true religious faith, plus faith's astonishing power to inspire acts of heroism. If this is not the case, then our belief is no more than a serious form of the absurd. All this must be expressed through situation and action, whether it be belief in humankind, or in science, or in both together. In order to simplify the issue I will say that mankind of old faced absurdity, and escaped it through religion. And today again, man faces absurdity; but how can he escape this time? It is pointless to entertain hopes of communicating with people in a language other than the one they use; and we have acquired a new language, which is science. This is the only language in which we can articulate greater and lesser truths. For they are the old truths after all, once contained in the language of religion; and they must now be re-presented in the new language of man.

Let us look to the scientists for example and method. It seems that they are never trapped by absurdity. Why? Perhaps because they have no time for it! Perhaps also because they are permanently in contact with reality. Relying on a successful methodology of proven worth, they are not assailed by doubt or despair. One among them may spend twenty years solving an equation; and the equation will provoke new interest, and consume new lifetimes of research, and thus another firm footstep will be taken along the path of truth. The abode of scientists smells sweet; it is the smell of progress, of success. Questions like "Where do we come from?" and "Where are

we going?" and "What is the meaning of life?" present
no temptation for them. They give no intimation of absurdity. Real knowledge provides an ethical system in an
age when morals are crumbling. It is manifested in a love
of truth; in integrity in judgment; in a monastic devotion
to work; in cooperation in research; and in a spontaneous
disposition toward an all-embracing, humanist attitude.
Is it possible, on the level of the particular, for scientific
excellence to replace opportunism in the hearts of the
new generation?

In any case, it is best for now that I occupy myself
no further with the theme. I shall return to it after a
summary of the other elements I need for the work.

I imagine the scenario to unfold in the following fashion:

A young woman launches an attack on a group of
men in order to change them. She must succeed in this
by way of art—if not, then the play has no meaning. A
serious woman and absurdist men. I require a love story.
It would be truly interesting if they were all to fall in
love with her and she had to choose one of them; or if
she should fall, without knowing it, in love with one of
them. There must be a dramatic tension between the love
interest and the problem of the serious and the absurd,
so that the play does not flag. But will it develop as a
love story within the framework of an intellectual con-
flict? Will it perhaps be confined to intellectual discussions
and whispered intimacies? And how, and when, will the
plot develop to a conclusion in an artistically convincing
way? Will it be based on debate or on emotion? I lack

some important, essential thing; what is it? How can absurdists find any kind of creed? And what is the extent of this creed? Is it enough for it to be a belief in society? I mean, is that sufficient for heroism to be created anew?

I am at least aware of the ideas that I must crystallize and clarify to construct a plot. I should now record some basic facts and observations about the characters in this scenario—under their own names, for the time being. Perhaps then I will be delivered from confusion, since it is possible that a plot may arise spontaneously if I can analyze them and determine their basic attributes.

CHARACTERS OF THE PLAY

(1) AHMAD NASR

A civil servant, by all accounts competent, with great experience in the practical matters of daily life. Happily married, with a teenage daughter, and religious, I think out of habit. All in all a normal person; I do not know how he will serve the aims of the play. But there is one important question: Why does he smoke the water pipe? Leaving aside what people say about sexual drives, is there something he is trying to escape? But in any case he must be created anew in the sense that he is, deep down, not convinced that his job and his family should take all his energy. In a corner of his mind, he feels that he is responsible. That he must be responsible for what goes on around him. And because he is a believer, he is the most well-balanced of all of them—but in spite of that, or perhaps because of that, it grieves him that he is a person of no consequence in life whatsoever. Thus we can consider his well-known concern with small problems—as we can his addiction—as a kind of escape from the feelings of absurdity that gnaw at him. He will entertain this secret misery unconsciously. On the outside, he will remain the steady person, the believer, the efficient and untroubled man—until the heroine shows him his true self, perhaps through his love for her.

(2) MUSTAFA RASHID

A lawyer. No harm in my leaving him as such in the play, to justify his powers of argument. Charming, and cynical in the extreme. Married to a woman he does not love—perhaps out of a desire for her salary more than anything else. Although he is constantly searching for an ideal woman, he does not in fact pursue erotic liaisons on the houseboat. He is a strange man, doubtless harboring some deep secret. Perhaps it is addiction. He is completely aware of his spiritual emptiness, and finds solace in the water pipe and the Absolute. But he is apparently unaware of the deception that he is practicing on himself. He strives for the impossible without any method or any real effort, relying solely on intoxicated meditations. It is as if the Absolute is simply an excuse for addiction, but gives him even so a feeling that he has risen above his real vapidity. Like many whom I meet at social gatherings, he is apparently exquisitely cultured but inwardly hollow, crumbling, stinking of his own miserable decay.

(3) ALI AL-SAYYID

Originally a student at al-Azhar University, he completed his studies thereafter at the Faculty of Arts at Cairo University, and perfected his English at a Berlitz language school. He is a combative character, and fully aware of his short-term, practical aims. He has two wives, the first from his village and the second from Cairo, but the latter is also a housewife and traditional woman—which satisfies his conservative inclinations to be the master of the house. He makes a lot of his generosity in keeping the first wife, but he is a swine, as can be seen by his strange relationship with Saniya Kamil.

As a critic, he is a great scoundrel. His aesthetic is founded on material gain, and he never feels compelled to tell the truth except when his fortunes turn against him, in which case it is disguised as mocking and merciless satire. Harried by feelings of worthlessness and treachery and futility, he devotes himself to the water pipe and to strange dreams of a new humanism which appear before his muzzy eyes through a lethal fog. He is the prime example of a certain contemporary type who wanders aimlessly through life without beliefs or morality. And who would not shrink from committing a crime if he could be sure that he would not be found out.

(4) KHALID AZZUZ

He inherited an apartment block, which means that he lives a life of ease in spite of the obvious mediocrity of his talent. He has found his escape in the water pipe and in sex—and in that gelatinous kind of literature whose degenerate promiscuity is appalling. It is difficult to determine whether his loss of belief—any belief—is what led him to this degenerate life, or whether the degeneracy drove him to reject his belief. For that reason I do not believe it impossible that one day he will return to his traditional faith when his creative spring dries up. Unlike his friends, he is completely idle; he takes from society and gives nothing back—nothing, that is, except stories like the tale of the piper whose pipe turns into a snake! Neither do I think it unlikely that he will be looking down at us one day from the balcony of the absurd.

(5) RAGAB AL-QADI

He is the hope of the drama. If he does not yield to development, then I can say farewell to the play. His father, according to Ali al-Sayyid, was a barber, and still plies his trade in the village of Kom Hammada in spite of his son's fame—either from his own pride or because of some meanness on the part of his son. Ragab is a race apart. One of those gods who die in their fifties. And as a god of passion, he is not without a harshness which can be made gentle only by love. Like the others, he is without belief or principles, but, unlike them, he displays a nervousness, a tension. Compellingly handsome, he is famous for his dark looks. His power is unlimited. His real release lies in sex; the water pipe appears not to affect him very much. His possibilities for the play do not need mentioning.

(5) ANIS ZAKI

Failed civil servant. Former husband and former father. Silent and dazed, morning and night. They say he is cultured; the only thing he has in the world is an extensive library. Sometimes he seems to me to be half mad, or half dead. He has managed to forget completely what it is he is escaping from. He has forgotten himself. His sturdy build betokens a strength that might have been. He can be described by any attribute—or none at all. He keeps his secret in his head. One can be sure of him in the same way that one can be sure of an empty chair. Useful for comic exploitation, but he will not play a positive role in the play.

I can confine the female characters to two: the heroine, because of the importance of her role, and Sana, to enhance the unity of sentiment in the drama. And also because her modern adolescent character lends an attractive spirit to the play, one not wholly without usefulness for study. And furthermore, the heroine's victory over her on the battlefield of love can be taken as a symbol of the victory of the Serious over the Absurd in the female domain; since there is no point to seriousness if its roots cannot penetrate womankind, who is after all the mother of the future.

Beyond that, there is no need for Saniya Kamil, who practices her own special brand of polyandry; or for the blond translating spinster, who imagines herself to be a pioneering martyr, whereas in fact she is a pioneer only in the incoherent depravity of addiction.

There was no more writing—just a heading: *Important Observations,* which was set alone in the middle of the line and was followed by a blank space. He turned over the succeeding pages until he reached the cover, but found not another word. He put the notebook in his pocket, muttering, "The little ...!" Then he took it out again and reread what was written about him, and then he put it back in his pocket. He laughed. He looked at the empty coffee cup. That won't be any good now, he thought. It would be a long wait. Perhaps he would still be clear-headed when the company gathered. Amm Abduh's voice echoed from the mosque as he made the call for sunset prayer. "The little ...!" he muttered again.

The houseboat shook with approaching footsteps. He looked toward the door, wondering who it could be who was coming so early.

And from behind the screen by the door appeared Samara Bahgat.

11 ⤆

She approached, greeting him with a forced smile, clearly preoccupied.

"You do not seem to be yourself," he said.

She paced around the room, looking high and low. "What's the matter?" he asked.

"I've lost some important things," she replied.

"Here?"

"I had them yesterday, during the evening."

"What are they?"

"A notebook for my work—and a small amount of money."

"Are you sure that you lost them here?"

"I'm not sure of anything."

"Amm Abduh sweeps up, and the man comes to take away the trash in the morning."

She sat down in an armchair. "If they were stolen," she said, "why didn't the thief take the whole bag? Why did he take the notebook and leave the purse?"

"Perhaps you dropped it."

"Anything's possible . . ."

"Can it not be replaced?"

Before she could reply, the houseboat shook again, and voices were heard outside. Hastily, she begged him to forget the matter, telling him not to mention it again as she went to take her place on the mattress. All the friends came in together, and soon the party was complete. Anis devoted himself earnestly and avidly to the water pipe; he was in an unfamiliar state of alertness. Deep inside him, the demons began to incite him to malice. He shot a cunning glance at Samara.

Mustafa was speaking to her. "It's all clear now. You come early to be alone with Anis!"

She played along. "Didn't you realize? He is my knight in shining armor!"

"We're only boys," commented Ahmad, "while he is a mature man in his forties."

Without being summoned, Amm Abduh appeared at the screened door. "A houseboat has sunk at Imbaba," he announced.

They turned toward him in concern. "Did anybody drown?" Ahmad asked.

"No—but they lost the entire contents of the boat."

"That's what we care about, the contents," said Khalid, "not the individuals!"

"And the rescue police came," continued Amm Abduh.

"The arts police should have come as well."

"Why did it sink?" asked Layla.

"The watchman was negligent," replied the old man.

"Or perhaps," added Khalid, "because the Almighty was angry about what went on inside."

They said amen to that, and turned again to the water pipe. When Amm Abduh had gone, Ali said: "One night I had a dream that I had become as tall and broad as Amm Abduh."

Anis broke his customary silence. "That's because you take refuge in dreams and addiction," he said.

They met his comment with laughter. "But taking refuge from what, O master of pleasures?" asked Ali.

"From your own emptiness!" replied Anis, and when the laughter had died down, he continued: "You are all modern-day scoundrels, escaping into addiction and groundless delusions..." And he turned and looked at Samara. The demons cackled inside him. A barrage of comments followed.

"At last he has spoken."

"A philosopher is born!"

All eyes were still turned on Anis. "And what about me?" Mustafa asked him.

"Escaping into addiction and the Absolute, you are hounded by the sense of your own worthlessness."

He could make out Samara's laughter among the roars of mirth, but avoided looking at her. He imagined her turmoil; he imagined her face; he imagined her innermost feelings—and then he continued: "We are all scum, we have no morals; we are pursued by a fearful demon by the name of Responsibility..."

"This night," said Ragab, "will go down in the annals of the houseboat."

Mustafa spoke again. "I bet tonight's kif has been smuggled from Moscow!"

"Anis! O philosopher!" It was Khalid's turn. "What about me—and Layla?"

"You are a depraved degenerate because you have no belief; or perhaps it's that you have no belief because you are depraved. As for Layla, she is a pioneer, but only in dissipation and addiction, not a martyr as she mistakenly believes."

"Hold your tongue!" shouted Layla.

But he merely pointed to Saniya, saying: "And you are a bigamist, you dope fiend!"

"You're mad!" screamed Saniya.

"No. Merely half mad. And also half dead."

"How dare you be so rude!"

Ali soothed her. "Now you are really angry, Saniya. He is the master of ceremonies, remember . . ."

"I will not be mocked in front of strangers!" she retorted.

The thunderous atmosphere threatened to overwhelm the merriment. Ragab, however, spoke firmly. "There are no strangers here. Samara is with us all the way."

"She may be with us, but only *all the way* with you!"

"No," said Anis. "She doesn't care about a man who flees from his own emptiness into addiction and sex."

"What a night we're having, boys!" cried Ragab gaily.

"Who would have thought that you were Anis the Silent?"

"Perhaps he's regurgitating one of his books—the decline of civilization, for example."

And there is still a bomb inside me—I'm saving it for the Director General. Let the laughter bursting inside me calm down, so that I can see things clearly. Have the mooring chains of the boat parted? The full moon charges at the fragile door of our balcony. As for the midges, I

understand at last their fatal fascination with the lamp-
light.

"You don't seem very happy," Ragab remarked to
Samara.

She spoke without looking at Saniya, but her listless
tone made it clear whom she meant. "That is how
strangers are, in company," she said.

"No, I won't have it," Ragab said. "Saniya is a lovely
woman—a kindly mother even when she's in love . . ."

"Thank you, Ragab," Saniya said benevolently.
"You're the best of all of us to make my apologies to
sister Samara."

"Let's not tie the knot of peace too firmly," said
Khalid. "It might get boring."

The only sound was the gurgling of the water pipe.
The ripples of sound spread out in the moonlight. His
racing pulse told him that sleep would be hard on this
tumultuous night. That he would experience the insomnia
of lovers without love. He began to recall all the verses
he knew from the poetry of demented lovers. The company disappeared, and he alone remained with the shining
night. He saw a horseman, his steed galloping through
the air just above the water's surface, and asked him who
he was. The rider replied that he was Omar Khayyam,
and that he had managed to escape death at last . . . He
awoke to the sight of his outstretched leg next to the
brass tray. Long and bony, pallid in the blue light. Hairy.
Big toes with nails curved over, so long had he gone
without cutting them. He could hardly believe that it was
his leg. Astonishing, the way one's own limb could seem

like that of a stranger . . . He realized that Mustafa was speaking. "Are we really as the master of ceremonies described, do you think?" he asked the company.

It was Khalid who replied. "It is not escape, or anything like that. We simply understand what we really are, as we should."

"This houseboat is the last refuge of human wisdom," added Ali.

"Is submerging yourself in dreams an escape?"

"The dreams of today are the realities of tomorrow."

"Is searching for the Absolute an escape?"

"What else can we do, for heaven's sake?"

"And is sex an escape?"

"It's creation itself, rather!"

"And what about the pipe—is that escape?"

"Escape from the police, if you like!"

"Is it escape from life?"

"It's life itself!"

"So why did our master of ceremonies attack us like that?"

"For ten years he's led a quiet life, with no need to make a stir of any kind. He didn't want to push his luck."

"And what a night it is, boys!"

Ahmad called for a little silence, so as not to dispel the delirium. The water pipe made its prescribed and unchanging round.

The moon had risen now beyond their field of vision. He was alone in having read the miserable defeat in Samara's eyes. Their faces appeared pale and sleepy, and serious as well, in spite of themselves. Mustafa fixed Samara with a quizzical look, and asked her her opinion on it all; but Ragab said: "The end of the night was not made for discussions."

What was it made for, then? They all left, save Ali and Saniya. It was not long before he was alone in the room. Amm Abduh came as he usually did and carried out his task without their exchanging a word, and then he left. Anis crawled out to the balcony, and saw the moon again, shining in the center of the studded dome of heaven. He spoke to it intimately. There is nothing like our houseboat, he murmured. Love is an old and worn-out game, but it is sport on the houseboat. Fornication is held as a vice by councils and institutions, but it is freedom on our houseboat. Women are all conventions and marriage deeds in the home, but they are nubile and alluring on the houseboat. And the moon is a satellite, dead and cold, but on the houseboat, it is poetry; and madness is everywhere an illness, but here it is philosophy, and something was something everywhere else but here; for here it was nothing. O, you ancient sage Ibur, summon for us your age, from which everything save poetry has melted away! Come and sing for us. Tell me what you said to the Pharaoh. Come, sage!

And the sage recited:

Your boon companions lied to you;
These years are full of war and tribulation.

I said: Recite again, sage! And he sang:

What is this which has come to pass in Egypt?
The Nile still brings its flood;
He who had nothing is rich now;
Would that I had raised my voice before.

What did you say also, sage?

You have wisdom and vision and justice,
But you let corruption gnaw at the land.
See how your orders are held in contempt!
Will you order till there comes one who will tell you the
truth?

12 ❧

He awoke to a voice whispering his name.

He opened his eyes to find himself lying on his back on the balcony. A shining halo in the sky betrayed the moon, now hidden from his gaze. Where was he—and in what time?

"Anis!"

He turned his head, and saw Samara standing on the threshold of the balcony. He sat up, leaning on his elbows, looking up at her, not fully awakened from the intoxication of his dreams.

"I am sorry to have come back at such an unsuitable time!"

"Is it still the same night?"

"It's only an hour since everyone left. I'm truly sorry."

He shuffled over to lean against the railing of the balcony, and tried to remember.

"I came back from Tahrir Square," she said, "after Ragab dropped me there."

"It's an honor, I'm sure. You can have my room if you deign to stay."

But she said, agitated: "I did not come back to sleep—as you know very well!" And then she added quietly, lowering her eyes: "I want my notebook."

"Your notebook!" he echoed, frowning.

"If you please."

The demons of malice awoke. "You are accusing me of theft!" he protested.

"No, I am not! But you came across it somehow."

"You mean that I stole it."

"I beg you, give it back to me—this is no time for talking!"

"You are mistaken."

"I am not mistaken!"

"I refuse to listen to any more of this accusation."

"I am not accusing you of anything. Give me back the notebook that I lost here."

"I don't know where it is."

"I heard you repeating what was written in it!"

"I don't understand."

"Oh yes, you do—you understand everything, and there is no reason to torment me."

"Tormenting people is not one of my hobbies."

"The night will soon be over."

"Will Mommy punish you if you get home late?" he teased her.

"Please, be serious, if only for a minute."

"But we don't know what the word means."

"Do you intend to tell everyone about it?" she asked anxiously.

"What have I to do with it, since I know nothing about it?"

"Please, be nice—I know you are, really."

"I am not 'nice.' I am half mad and half dead."

"What is written in the notebook—it's not my opinion of you—just a summary of thoughts I'm preparing for a play..."

"We're back in the world of riddles and accusations."

"I am still hoping that you will behave honorably."

"What has given you this idea, anyway?" he demanded.

"You repeated my words verbatim!"

"Don't you believe in coincidences?"

"I do believe that you will give me back my book!"

"In that case, you'd succeed in understanding in days what I have failed to in years!" And his laugh broke the silence of the void over the Nile. Then he said, in a new tone: "Your observations are inane, believe me."

"So you admit it!" she cried, gratified.

"I will give it back to you, but it will be no good for anything."

"It is nothing more than some basic ideas—they have not been developed yet."

"But you are a ... vile girl."

"God forgive you ..."

"You came not for friendship, but for snooping around!"

"Don't think so badly of me!" she protested. "I truly like you all, and I want to be your friend—and besides, I believe that there is a real hero in every individual. I was not interested in getting to know you just to use you in a play!"

"Don't bother to make excuses. It doesn't interest me at all, in fact."

He held out his hand to her. The notebook was in it. "As for the fifty piasters," he said. "I think I'll owe them to you."

She was perplexed. "But how?...I mean..."

"How did I steal the money? It's a terribly simple matter. We consider everything we come across on the boat to be public property!"

"I beg you—give me an explanation to set my mind at rest."

"I just couldn't resist it!" he said, laughing.

"Did you need the money?"

"Of course not. I'm not as poor as that."

"Then why did you take it?"

"I found, in spending it in the way that I did, that I could have a kind of closeness to you."

"Really, I don't understand at all."

"Neither do I."

"But I have begun to doubt my whole plan..."

"It's better that you don't have one at all." She laughed. "Except one that will lead you to the one you desire!" he went on, and she laughed again. "I understand you," he said, "just as everyone here understands you."

She was about to leave, but when he spoke she stood still, intrigued.

"You are only here because of Ragab," he said.

She laughed scornfully, but he pointed to the bedroom. "Careful not to wake the lovers."

"I am not what you think! I am a girl who..."

"If you really are a girl," he interrupted, "then come to my room and prove it!"

"How sweet you are—but you wouldn't care for me."

"Why?"

"Because it is too much if the girl is serious."

"But I only ever invite serious girls!"

"Really?"

"All the street girls are serious."

"God forgive you!"

"They don't know what absurdity is. They work until the crack of dawn, and there's no fun or pleasure in it. But they have a truly progressive aim—and that is to lead better lives!"

"Shame on you all! None of you can tell the difference between seriousness and frivolity!"

"Seriousness and frivolity are two names for the same thing."

She sighed, indicating that she was about to depart, but hesitated for a moment. "Will you tell the others about the notebook?" she asked.

"If that were my intention, I would have done it."

"I beg you, by all that is dear, tell me frankly what you have in mind."

"I have."

"I would prefer simply to disappear rather than be driven away."

"I do not want either to happen."

They shook hands in farewell. "Thank you," she said, like a close friend.

As she hurried away, the voice of Amm Abduh rang out, giving the call to the dawn prayer.

13 ❧

The houseboat rocked; someone was coming. Since the party was already complete, they wondered who it could be, and looked toward the door with a certain anxiety. Ahmad rose in order to stop the newcomer at the door, but a familiar laugh was heard, and then Sana's voice, calling: "Hello!" She came in, bringing by the hand a well-dressed young man. Ragab stood up to welcome him, saying: "Good evening, Ra'uf!" and introduced him to the others as "the well-known film star . . ." The couple sat down amidst lukewarm and formal expressions of greeting.

Sana said, in a voice that was bolder than usual: "He gave me so much trouble before he finally agreed to come! He said: 'How can we intrude on their privacy?' But he is my fiancé—and you are all my family!"

She received congratulations from all the group, and continued: "And like you, he's one of those!"—pointing at the water pipe and laughing. Her breath smelled of drink. Anis felt no embarrassment, and vigorously sent the pipe on its rounds. "Aren't you lucky, Ra'uf," Sana said next. "Here is the great critic Ali al-Sayyid, and the famous writer Samara Bahgat—the pipe makes strange bedfellows!"

"But Samara, unfortunately, does not partake," said Ragab.

"Why does she keep on coming, then!" Sana replied scornfully.

Ra'uf whispered a few words in her ear that were unintelligible to anyone else; she only giggled. Then Amm Abduh came in to change the water in the pipe, and when he had gone, Sana said to Ra'uf: "Can you believe that all that great hulk is one man?" And she laughed again, but this time alone. There followed a tense silence that lasted a quarter of an hour. Finally Ra'uf prevailed upon her to leave with him. Taking her by the arm, he stood up. "My apologies," he said. "We must go—we have an urgent appointment. I am very happy to have met you all . . ."

Ragab accompanied them to the door, and then returned to his seat. They remained gloomy in spite of the water pipe passing from hand to hand. Ragab smiled at Samara to humor her, but she only said, indicating the pipe and alluding to Sana's scornful remark, "Whatever I say, no one believes me."

"It doesn't disgrace you totally to have people say that," said Layla.

"Except when those people are my enemies."

"You have no enemies," said Ragab simply, "except the fossilized remnants of the bourgeoisie."

But she began to talk about the rumors that were spreading among her journalist colleagues, and she mentioned also her former flat in al-Manyal, where her late homecomings had set the neighbors to gossiping. "And when my mother said: 'Her job keeps her out late,' they said: 'Well, what keeps her at her job!'"

"But you are living on Kasr el-Aini Street now," said Ragab.

Mustafa tried to arouse Anis; a repeat of yesterday's outburst might disperse the gloom. But Anis did not come out of his own world. He was thinking of the empty cycles that hemmed him in every day; the rising and the setting of sun and moon, going out to and returning from the Ministry, friends gathering and parting, wakefulness and sleep. Those cycles that reminded him of the end and made something into nothing. Fathers and grandfathers had turned in these revolutions, and the earth waited calmly for their hopes and pleasures to fertilize its soil. What does it matter, that passions are consumed by fire, turned to clouds of smoke tainted with the musk of a forbidden and obscure magic . . .

As for Layla, she tormented herself with a fruitless love, soaring out into the void like a spaceship out of orbit. The god of sex stretches out his leg until his white shoe comes to rest against the brazier, and he stares at this delightful and irksome girl, his gaze smoldering in his compelling black eyes. There was much said on the subject of Sana and her fiancé, but Ragab did not share in it. When the friends noticed his total absorption in Samara, Rashid said: "How fortunate we are, to witness in our age the story of a grand passion."

"Oh, let's call it by its real name," said Khalid.

"Don't spoil the dream for us!" pleaded Ahmad.

"What is new about it," said Layla, "is that one of the parties is a serious person."

"What could be the role of a serious woman in love whose lover is futile?" wondered Khalid.

"Cathartic," Ragab replied. "To purify him of his futility."

"And if his futility were his unchanging essence?"

"Love must be victorious in the end!" said Ragab, and Samara laughed at them all.

Khalid spoke. "I would be interested to see a serious girl in love. A minister tripping up is so much funnier than an acrobat."

"There is no difference between a serious and a frivolous woman when it comes to love," said Ali. "Seriousness is simply a practical concern with public matters in the same way as private ones."

Khalid winked in the direction of Samara. "In which of the two regards," he inquired, "do you think she is concerned now?" At which everybody laughed, and then he continued: "Do you think there is any hope of her becoming interested in general concerns?"

"Her hopes are pinned on the new generation!"

Khalid looked at Ragab. "It appears that the generation of the forties is no longer good for anything but love," he said.

"That is, if it *is* actually any good at love!"

"The new generation is better than us," said Ahmad.

"Is there no hope for our changing, then?" asked Mustafa.

"We usually change only in plays and films," said Khalid. "And that is our weakness."

"And the strength of the satires which show us our true selves!" said Ali.

"Why don't you ever admit to that in your articles?"

"Because I am a hypocrite," said Ali, "and I was

referring anyway to foreign comedies. As for the home-grown versions, they usually end in a sudden character change on the part of the lead in a facile, preachy manner. That's why the third act is usually the weakest in the play; it is usually written for the censors."

Khalid turned to Samara. "If you were thinking of writing a play about people like us, then I would advise you as a fellow writer to choose the comic form. I mean farce or absurdism—they're the same thing."

"That is certainly worth considering," said Samara, continuing to ignore Ragab's gaze.

"Avoid the committed type of hero who does not smile, or speak, except of the higher ideal, who exhorts people to do this or that, who loves sincerely, and sac-rifices himself, and pronounces slogans, and finally kills the audience off because he is so insufferable!"

"I will take your advice," Samara said. "I will write instead about those others who kill off the audience be-cause they are so charming!"

"But these also have their artistic problems," Khalid continued. "They live without any beliefs at all, wasting their time in futile pursuits in order to forget that they will soon turn into ashes and bones and nitrogen and water; and at the same time they are worn down by a daily life that forces upon them a certain kind of desperate and—to them—meaningless seriousness. Don't forget, either, that the insane everywhere around us threaten destruction at any moment. People like this do not act, they do not develop; so how can you hope to succeed in constructing a play around them?"

"That's the question!"

"And then there is another problem, which is that any one of them is no different from any other—except in outer appearance. That is, any one of them is not a personality, but is made up from disintegrating elements, like a crumbling building. We can distinguish between one house and another, but how can we tell the difference between two piles of stones, wood, glass, concrete, mortar, dust, paint? They are like modern painting, one canvas just like the next. So how can you justify having several characters on the stage?"

"You are practically telling me to give up writing!"

"Not at all—but I am pointing out that like attracts like. Just as the righteous stick together and the evil find each other, so is the drama of the absurd for the absurdists. Brother Ali here will never take you to task for the lack of plot or character or dialogue. No one will embarrass you with questions about the meaning of this or that. Since there is no foundation to build on, your detractors cannot shake you. Indeed, you will find people who will praise you work, who will say—and rightly—that you have expressed, through a chaotic play, a world whose identity is chaos . . ."

"But we do not live in a world whose identity is chaos!"

Khalid sighed. "And that is the difference between you and me. You can go back to the loving looks of brother Ragab now."

Nothing here turns with certainty, sure of its goal; nothing save the pipe. Before long, lethargy will descend from its enchanted abode among the stars and tongues will be stilled. The new passion will likely bear fruit before the night is out in the form of a kiss beneath the guava tree. And before that, the earth has turned for millions and millions of years to result in this night party on the surface of the Nile. The moon disappeared from view, but he could see the gecko above the balcony door. It ran, and then stopped, and then ran again. It seemed as if it was looking for something. "Why is there movement?" he asked.

They turned to him, expecting some surprise.

"What movement, master of ceremonies?" asked Mustafa.

And he murmured, continuing with his work: "Any movement at all."

14 ❧

As it was an official holiday, Anis spent the day on the balcony and in the sitting room, withdrawn into a state of complete harmony. Just before sunset Amm Abduh came to prepare for the evening. He bid Anis a happy festival day for the third or fourth time, thinking that it was the first time he had greeted him. Anis asked him what he knew about the festival. Amm Abduh replied that it was on this day that the Prophet left the unbelievers—curses upon them—for a new place.

"This room will shortly be filled with unbelievers!" said Anis.

The old man laughed, unable to credit such a thing.

"You are escaping into your faith," Anis continued wickedly.

"Escaping!" Amm Abduh replied. "I came here one day, a long time ago, riding on top of a train."

"Where did you come from!"

"Oh . . ."

"And from what crime were you fleeing?"

"Well . . ."

He was determined to forget. Perhaps he really had come to Cairo on the run from some crime. Perhaps he was carried to the city on the wave of revolution in 1919. And now he no longer knew; and so no one knew at all.

"Are you a serious man, Amm Abduh?" he asked, still teasing.

"Ah!"

"Do you not know that Samara is a new Prophet?"

"Almighty God forgive you!"

"And she has an army behind her, to wage war on Nothingness, and march forward!"

"Where to?" asked the simple Amm Abduh.

"To prison—or to the madhouse."

Amm Abduh left for the sunset prayer. "Where shall I find a cat for all the rats on the embankment?" he murmured to himself as he left.

The friends arrived shortly afterward, earlier than usual in celebration of the holiday. Anis set about his usual business. They talked, for some of the time, about their personal affairs. Ragab announced that he planned to raise his asking fee to five thousand pounds per film, and Khalid congratulated him, for reaffirming in this way his loyalty to Arab socialism. Ragab laughed, but made no comment. He began instead to talk about Sana, how she was appearing with Ra'uf at parties and at the studios as his fiancée. Ragab was sure that this engagement would not end in marriage. Layla wondered how long the serious one's seat would remain unoccupied.

"She came back yesterday from a press tour of the industrial zone," Ali said. "She will probably come tonight."

"Tell us the truth," said Khalid to Ragab. "What is your relationship with her?"

Ragab smiled.

"Are you meeting in some little bachelor apartment behind our backs?" Khalid pursued.

"Certainly not—you must believe me! There are no secrets between us here!"

"In that case, you must now admit defeat for the first time in your life."

"Not at all. I'm just not launching my attack quite yet, so I can relive my memories of Platonic love!"

"So there is love?"

"Of course."

"On your part as well?"

He took a deep drag on the pipe, and exhaled in a leisurely fashion. "I am not devoid of love," he said at last.

"Love, Ragab style?" Saniya inquired.

"Yes, but a new model."

"This means that it is essentially nothing."

"Let's wait and see."

"She is truly beautiful," Ahmad said.

"But she has a strong personality," said Ali.

"Which is a somewhat repellent characteristic in a woman," said Saniya, at which Layla fixed her with a disapproving look, so she cheerfully amended: "Well, it can be, sometimes."

"The more impregnable the fortress, the greater the glory of those who take her," said Ragab.

"But the atom bomb takes no account of fortresses or conquerors," said Layla.

"She has turned down a splendid marriage," said Ahmad. "That deserves admiration in itself."

"Don't prejudge the matter!" said Saniya. She turned to Ragab. "Has she not referred to marriage at all?"

"Sometimes marriage comes without anyone referring to it, like death," he replied.

"Tell me truly, could you seriously contemplate marriage?"

He paused for a moment before saying: "No." His hesitation made a deep impression on everyone. Why don't I put the brazier out on the balcony and have my own fire festival? Its blaze is immortal, unlike that of false stars. But women are like the dust, known not only by their rich scent but by the way they seep and settle into you. Cleopatra, for all her amours, never divulged the secret of her heart. The love of a woman is like political theater: there is no doubt about the loftiness of its goal, but you wonder about the integrity of it. No one benefits from this houseboat like the rats and the cockroaches and the geckos. And nothing bursts in unannounced through your door like grief. And yesterday the dawn said to me when it broke that really it had no name.

He listened to them discussing domestically produced meat and Russian fish and hard currency and the balance of payments. Then they all roared with laughter; and the boat shook, announcing a newcomer. Silence reigned. "Here comes the bride!" Saniya murmured.

Samara sauntered gaily in, and shook hands with them warmly as a festival greeting. She was eagerly asked about the trip, and replied that it was splendid, and that they should all go on one like it in order to be created anew. Khalid let his eyes wander over those present and then wondered aloud: "Do you think we *could* be created anew?"

They exchanged looks, and then were convulsed with laughter. "It's your fault!" Mustafa said. "You have failed to reveal the secret of your seriousness and zeal!"

"I will not fall into that trap!"

"It is clear that you are of the old faith like us, and—also like us—of the class that is sliding toward the abyss. So how, in the light of that, have you come upon the meaning of life? Won't you tell us at least what it is?"

She hesitated for a moment, and then said: "It's life itself that is important, not the meaning."

"But we feel life propelling us along instinctively, and within those bounds, we lead it perfectly well."

"No!"

"We've already told you—"

She interrupted him. "Some of us have an instinctive death wish, as you well know!"

"And the way out?"

"Is to come out of your shell."

"Pretty talk, but it makes no difference one way or the other."

"Life is above logic."

And at that point Ragab said to her: "Careful—you're falling into the trap again!"

Amm Abduh came to change the water in the water pipe. Ali congratulated him on the good quality of the kif.

"Yesterday the dealer advised me to buy enough for a month. He says the police are watching him," Amm Abduh said.

"That's just a ploy to fleece us. Take no notice."

"Amm Abduh," Samara asked him, "aren't you afraid of the police?"

Mustafa replied for him. "He's so long in the tooth," he said, "that he is above the law."

A star twinkled on the horizon like a serene smile. Anis asked it about the police; were they really watching the dealer? It replied that they watched the wakeful, not the drugged; and that stars twinkled as they approached the earth, and dimmed as they plunged further into space; and that some of the lights which adorned the dome of the heavens came from stars now shrouded in Nothingness; and that the power which subjects you to Nothingness is stronger than that which subjects you to Being. A comet suddenly plummeted down, so close that he imagined that it had landed on the violets on the bank, just beyond the houseboat.

"The whole department received a bonus for the festival except me," he said.

Ahmad Nasr cursed the Director General.

"I leaped up to protest, but burst out laughing instead," Anis finished.

They all laughed, but he shrugged his shoulders. Ali recalled how they used to celebrate this festival out at the Nile Barrages. Ragab said: "The best way to celebrate the Prophet's journey is to make one of our own." His face lit up. "What do you say to a trip to the country in my car?"

"But we haven't smoked enough yet!"

Samara thought it was a good idea. Ahmad said that

there was blessing to be had from a journey. Nobody objected—except Anis, who muttered: "No!"

But would the expedition proceed in two cars? No, in one; otherwise there would be no point. How, if the car only has room for seven and we are nine? Well, Layla can sit on Khalid's lap, and Saniya on Ali's. Enthusiasm for this spontaneous expedition grew. And Anis still said, languidly: "No . . ."

But they were bent on him coming. How could an adventure like this take place without the master of ceremonies? He refused to move, or to change his clothes, so they insisted on taking him in the long tunic he always wore at home. At about midnight, they rose to leave. Anis yielded under duress.

They went out toward the car. It was earlier than their usual time for leaving. Amm Abduh, who was standing in front of his hut like a palm tree, asked if he should go and tidy the room now. Anis told him to leave everything as it was until they returned.

15 ❧

The car set off, Ragab, Samara, and Ahmad sat in front, and the rest were squashed together in the back like one flattened body with six heads. They made for Pyramids Road, crossing the almost deserted city. Ragab suggested that the road to Saqqara would make a nice trip and everybody concurred, whether they knew the road or not. Anis sat hunched and silent in his white robe, pressed against the right-hand side of the car.

They covered Pyramids Road in minutes, and then turned left toward Saqqara. They began to travel at speed down the dark and deserted road, the headlights picking out the landmarks ahead. The road stretched infinitely out into the darkness, bordered on either side by great evergreens whose branches met overhead. On both sides lay the open spaces, the landscape and the air of the country. To their left the scenery was cut across by a canal running alongside the road. The water's surface stood out here and there under the faint starlight, iron gray against the black. The car went faster; the air rushed in, dry and refreshing and smelling of greenery. "Slow down," said Saniya to Ragab.

"Don't break the smokers' speed limit," said Khalid.

"Are you a speed freak?" Samara asked him.

We are on the way to the site of an ancient Pharaonic

tomb. A good moment to recite the opening verse of the
Qur'an . . .

Ragab soon slowed down again. Khalid suggested
that they stop for a while and go for a stroll in the dark.
Everybody agreed, so Ragab turned off onto a dusty patch
of ground between two trees, and stopped the car. Doors
were opened. Ahmad, Khalid, Saniya, Layla, Mustafa, and
Ali got out. Anis shifted himself away from the car door
and sat comfortably for the first time. He shook out his
tunic and stretched his legs. He searched with one foot
for the slipper he had lost in the crush. When they called
him to go with them, he replied tersely: "No."

Ragab caught hold of Samara's hand as she was about
to get out. "We can't leave the master of ceremonies
alone," he said.

The expedition moved off. They were going toward
the canal, laughing and talking. They turned into phan-
toms in the starlight, and then disappeared altogether,
leaving only disembodied voices.

"What is the meaning of this journey?" asked Anis
thickly.

"It's the journey that is important," Ragab teased,
"not the meaning."

Samara said: "Hmm!"—in protest at his allusion to
her; but Anis was complaining now. "The darkness
makes me sleepy," he grumbled.

"Enjoy it, master of ceremonies," said Ragab eagerly.
Then he turned to Samara. "We must talk about us," he
said. "Honestly. Like the honesty of the nature surround-
ing us."

It is difficult to sleep when you are witnessing a romantic comedy. Very fitting, honesty, in the middle of the night on the road to Saqqara! Now his arm is creeping along the back of her seat. Anything can happen on the road to Saqqara.

"Yes," he continued. "Let us talk about our love."

"*Our* love?"

"Yes, ours! That is exactly what I meant!"

"It is not possible for me to have anything to do with a god."

"It is not possible that our lips have not yet become acquainted."

She turned her head away toward the fields as if to listen to the crickets and frogs. How beautiful the stars were over the fields, she murmured. I wonder if any new ideas have been recorded in the notebook. Could we still perhaps see ourselves one night on the theater stage, and guffaw along with the audience?

"I know what you would like to say," Ragab went on.

"What?"

"That you are not like the other girls."

"Is that what you think?"

"But love . . ."

"But love?"

"You don't believe me!"

Where is honesty in this darkness? What do our voices mean to the insects? You are in your forties, Ragab. You'll have to start playing different roles soon. Do you not know how the great Casanova hid in the Duke's library?

"Please don't say 'bourgeois mentality' again," she said now.

"But how else can I interpret your fear?"

"I'm not afraid."

"Then it's a problem of trust?"

"I heard you say that in a film."

"Perhaps I don't believe in seriousness yet, but I believe in you."

"That's the Don Juan mentality!" she replied.

Ghosts, walking abroad in the fields—or in my head. Like the village in days gone by. Marriage, fatherhood, ambitions, death. The stars have lived for billions of years, but they have not yet heard of the stars of the earth. No ghosts out there; just lone trees, forgotten in the midst of the fields.

"I could perhaps remain chaste until we get married," Ragab was saying now.

"Get married?"

"But I have a devil in me that rebels against routine."

"Routine!"

"One hint, and you understand everything! But I do not understand you . . ."

Where is the balcony, and the lapping of the waves? The water pipe, and the smell of the river? Where is Amm Abduh? And those thoughts that gleam like lightning striking the shades of the evergreens and then vanish, but where?

"Why did you refuse to marry your important suitor?"

"I was not satisfied with him."

"You mean, you did not love him."

"If you like."

"He was in his forties, like me."

"It wasn't that."

"Satisfaction is only important in free choice. Not in love."

"I don't know."

"And sex?"

"That's a question that should properly be ignored!"

With a voice that broke the spell of the night, Anis shouted: "Rulings and classifications of age and love and sex? You damn grammarians!"

They turned around uncomfortably—and then both laughed. "We thought you were asleep," said Ragab.

"How long will we stay in this prison?"

"We've only been here an hour."

"Why haven't we committed suicide?"

"We were trying to talk about love!"

Across the abyss of the night came the voices of the expedition. Then their scattered shapes could be made out. They approached the car to stand together around the hood. Yes, my dear, we could easily have been killed out there . . . Where are they now, the days of knights and troubadours? Khalid said that he had been about to commit the primary sin, had the "fraudulent pioneer" not been so prudish.

"And then in the dark," Mustafa added, "we decided to find out how modern we really are, and see who could admit to the most misdeeds!"

Ragab thought it was a clever idea. "And so everyone confessed to their sins," continued Mustafa.

"Sins!"

"I mean, what are considered such in public opinion."

"And what was the outcome?"

"Wonderful!"

"How many could be called crimes?"

"Dozens."

"And how many were misdemeanors?"

"Hundreds!"

"Have none of you committed a virtue?"

"He who goes by the name of Ahmad Nasr!"

"Perhaps you mean his fidelity to his wife."

"And to financial directives and stocktaking and regulations for the acquisition of goods!"

"And what was your opinion of yourselves?"

"Our consensus was that we are in a state of nature, immaculate; and that the morals which we lack are the dead morals of a dead age; and that we are the pioneers of a new and honest ethic as yet unsanctioned by legislation!"

"Bravo!"

Anis gave himself over to the view of the trees that bordered the road. They had been planted with extraordinary regularity. If they moved out of their fixed order, the known world would come tumbling down. There was a snake coiled around a branch; it wanted to say something. Very well, say something worth listening to. But what a cursed row. "Let me hear it!" he cried aloud.

At his bellow, they all laughed.

"What do you want to hear?" asked Mustafa.

They piled back into the car, and Anis was once more

pressed against the door. The snake had completely disappeared.

"You will be driven by a thoroughly modern driver!" Ragab said. The car moved onto the road, engine roaring, and then they set off, faster and faster, until they were traveling at an insane speed.

People laughed hysterically; then their voices shook; and then they began to protest and shout for help. The trees flew by. They felt as if they were plummeting into a deep gulf, and waited in dread to hit the bottom.

"Madness—this is madness!"

"He'll kill us in cold blood!"

"Stop! We have to get our breath back!"

"No! No! Even madness has to stop somewhere!"

But Ragab put his head back in a terrifying frenzy, and drove as fast as the car would go, whooping like a Red Indian. Samara was forced to put a hand on his arm, and whisper: "Please!"

"Layla's crying," Khalid snapped. "Will you return to your senses!"

My mind is dead. All that is left in my head is the pulse of my blood. My heart is sinking as in the worst depressions of kif—close your eyes—that way you will not see death—

Suddenly a horrifying scream rang out. He opened his eyes, shaking, to see a black shape flying through the air. The car was jolted with the shock and nearly turned over, and they were thrown against the seats and doors by Ragab's violent braking. Sobs and cries of "God forbid!" broke out.

"Somebody was hit!"

"Killed ten times over."

"We should have seen this coming!"

"God, what an appalling night!"

"Get a grip on yourselves!" Ragab shouted. He pushed himself up in his seat and turned to look out through the back window. Then he sat down again and started to drive off. Ahmad leaned toward him, a question on his lips. "We must get out of here!" Ragab said decisively.

There was a sick silence. "It's the only solution!" he continued.

Nobody uttered a word. Then Samara whispered: "Perhaps he needs help?"

"He's already finished."

She said, this time more loudly: "You can't just . . . lay down the law like this!"

"What can we do, anyway! We are not doctors!"

"Well, what do you all think?" said Samara, turning to the others. And when not a word was said, she began: "I think—"

Ragab furiously slammed on the brakes. The car stopped in the middle of the road. Then he turned to the others. "Let no one say tomorrow that I took this decision into my own hands. I leave it up to you. What do you think we should do?" And then, when there was silence, he shouted: "Answer me! I promise you that I will do whatever you tell me!"

"We must get out of here!" said Khalid. "It's the only solution. If anyone disagrees, let them say so now."

"Get moving," Mustafa said anxiously. "Otherwise there's no hope."

Layla was still crying, which made Saniya start as well. At that point, Ragab turned to Samara. "As you see," he said, "we have a consensus."

And when she said nothing, he started off.

"We're living in the world," he said. "Not in a play."

They set off at a slow and steady pace. He drove woodenly, tense and thunderous. A funereal silence reigned. Anis closed his eyes, only to see the black shape flying through the air. Was he still perhaps in pain? Or did he not know why, and how, he had been killed? Or why he existed? Or was he finished forever? Did life just pass away, as if it had never been?

They drove without stopping until they reached the houseboat. They got out of the car without speaking. Ragab stayed behind to look at the hood of the car. Amm Abduh rose to greet them, but no one paid him any attention. Their faces looked pallid and devastated in the light of the blue lamp. It was not long before Ragab joined them, his features set hard in a way that they had not seen before.

When the silence became intolerable, Ali said: "It could perhaps have been an animal . . ."

"That scream was human," replied Ahmad.

"Do you think the investigation will lead to us?"

"We'll only lose sleep over that idea."

"And it was accidental," muttered Ragab.

"But to run away is a crime," said Samara.

"We had no option!" he said harshly. "And the de-

cision was unanimous!" And he began to pace back and
forth between the balcony and the door. Then he said:
"I am desolate . . . but it is best that we forget the whole
thing."

"If only we could!"

"We must forget; any other action would ruin the
reputation of three ladies, and confound the rest of us—
and send me straight to court."

Amm Abduh came. They looked at him in irritation,
but he did not notice anything unusual. "Do you need
anything?" he asked.

Ragab signaled him to go. He left the room, saying
that he was going to the mosque.

After he had gone, Ragab asked: "Do you think the
old man understood anything?"

"He understands nothing," Anis replied.

"We should all leave now," said Ragab nervously.

"Khalid agreed. "Dawn is about to break."

Khalid, Layla, Ali, Saniya, Mustafa, and Ahmad left.

Ragab turned to Samara. "I am sorry to have caused
you such distress," he said, "but come with me now, so
that I can take you home."

She shook her head in revulsion. "Not in that car."

"You don't believe in ghosts, surely!"

"No—but it was me it ran over . . ."

"Don't let your imagination run away with you!"

"It's true. I'm . . . shattered."

"All the same, I won't leave you. We can walk together until you find a taxi." And he stood in front of
her, waiting for her to rise to her feet.

16 ❧

The voice of Amm Abduh, making the dawn call to prayer, came to him; and he thought: I am alone. I should call someone to be with me, or go to be with someone.

He gestured with his arm at the night, and thought: The mystery has evaporated from my head and I am sober. He laughed at the extraordinary idea. But he was sober; and here was the coming dawn without a single voice talking, and there was no trace of the whale. Where was the rest of that fine stuff they had put in the pipe— run over by a car? The Caliph al-Hakim had murdered so many. When he came to believe that he was a god, he forbade the people to eat *mulukhiya*. Why did I give in and go out with them? So have I been crowned a killer. The speed, the madness, the murder, the escape; the sharp discussion, the taking of votes in bloodstained democracy. My wife and child rose and died once more. No one save the dead will sleep tonight. That scream, which mocked the perfection of the heavenly spheres! Unknown, from unknown to unknown. When would his mind have mercy on itself and surrender to sleep? The Caliph al-Hakim went up on the mountain to practice his sublime secrets, and did not return. He has not returned to this day. No trace of him has been found, but they still look for him now. That is why I say that he is alive. A blind man saw him once, but no one believed him. He might yet appear to those who smoke the pipe on the night that marks the Qur'an's revelation. As for that unknown man, he has murdered sleep.

His distracted gaze lingered on the refrigerator, just above the door. For the first time he discovered the resemblance between the curve of the door and the forehead of Ali al-Sayyid. And it had eyes as well, filled with tears of mirth. They said that the Caliph al-Hakim had been killed. Impossible. A man such as he could not be killed. But he could, if he wished, commit suicide. From the top of the mountain, he had looked down on Cairo, and commanded the mountain to crush the city; and when the mountain did not carry out his command he realized that his struggle was absurd, and killed himself. That is why I say that he is alive, and may still appear to those who smoke the pipe on the Night of Revelation . . .

He heard Amm Abduh's voice now, from the garden, as he was returning from the prayer. "In the name of God, the Merciful, the Compassionate," he was murmuring. Anis called him, and the old man came at once. "Aren't you asleep yet?" he said.

"Have you taken the rest of that good kif?" Anis asked him.

"No, I have not!"

"I've looked for it everywhere; I don't know where it has gone."

"Why are you still awake?"

"My head is still spinning from that damned trip."

"You must go to sleep. It will soon be morning."

As the old man started to leave, Anis asked him: "Amm Abduh, have you ever killed anyone in your life?" "Oh!"

Anis sighed vexedly. "Oh, go away," he said.

He began to pace to and fro to tire himself out. He went out to the balcony and threw himself down on a mattress, but he was so keenly awake that he despaired of sleep. The fact that there was no kif on the houseboat redoubled his anxiety and sense of foreboding. He would have to summon the patience of the stars.

The streetlights went out. Nature took on her true colors. The first glow of dawn came creeping, staining the horizon with a violet that deepened into carnation. Then the gloom retreated, and the acacias were born again. He rose to his feet, at once despairing and defiant. He held his head under the tap for a long time, and then drank a glass of milk, which he did not want, from the refrigerator. Then he made himself some coffee and sipped it. He became sick of the place; he put on his suit and left the houseboat early, to wander in the side streets until it was time to go to the office.

He came out to the street clearheaded for the first time. He felt as far as could be from the laughter, the reveries and apparitions of the pipe. The road stretched out ahead of him, bordered on both sides by tall trees. The tops of the trees bowed to meet one another, like a frown on the edge of his field of vision. For the first time he saw the houseboats; large and small, they were moored all along a shore made pretty by the variety of the gardens on the bank.

It was extraordinary. Each houseboat had its own personality, color, youth—or old age; its own human faces appearing at the windows. And the most astonishing thing, a date palm laden with yellow dates. He would not have believed that there was a single date palm on the bank. There were a great number of trees of different sizes and shapes and blossoms. He did not know their names, or anything about them.

A caravan of camels passed him. There was a man driving them. He wondered where they had come from, and where they were going. An intimation as strong as certainty stole into his mind: that he was sliding into a depression filled with tension and pain. There was a sign over the door of one of the houseboats: "Furnished Rooms to Let." So here was an empty flat, and a woman as well, not so old or unattractive either, looking in his direction from the upper floor of the houseboat. Think of all the possibilities awaiting a new, bachelor tenant. But how on earth did the sober man get through the day? There was a tree in his way; the huge, sturdy trunk stopped him short. He looked up at the branches spreading out in the breeze, a huge dome, the top lost in the thin, low clouds of the morning. Then he turned once more to the aged trunk, letting his gaze wander down to the splayed gray roots driving deep into the earth beneath the pavement like talons, as if the tree were in a rigid frenzy of defiance and pain. A patch of bark had been eaten away to reveal pale yellow inner wood, hollowed in the shape of a Gothic arch. Directly in front of him, as tall as he was, it invited him to go in. The great life

span of that tree—that one alone—would be enough to
convince anyone, even those who did not need to be
convinced, that plants were beings with no intelligence.
He walked on, examining everything around him, wondering amazed whether the color of existence was red or
yellow, and whether the bark of a tree was like a dead
man's skin—but when did I see the skin of a dead man?
Now he was sure that there was something in his way,
challenging, resisting, causing pain. He realized suddenly
that he had not shaved. And that when he had been
smoking he never forgot to shave. And that made matters
even more complicated. A voice asked him the time, but
he did not bother to answer it, and paid no attention. He
continued sluggishly on, catching sight of a morning
newspaper seller, and passing him by.

He had not read a newspaper for a long time; he
knew nothing of current events except what he picked
up from his friends' delirious commentaries that merged
into the endless babble of the smoking party. Who were
the ministers? What were the policies? How were things
going? But who cares! As long as you can walk along a
deserted street without a thug attacking you, as long as
Amm Abduh brings you the good stuff every evening,
as long as there is plenty of milk in the refrigerator, then
things must be going well. As for the agonies of sobriety,
car accidents, the cryptic conversations of the night, he
still did not know who was responsible for those affairs.

He arrived at the Ministry early. Hardly had he sat
down on his wooden chair when he was overcome by
an irresistible desire for sleep. He rested his head on the

desk and sank into a deep slumber. His colleagues called on him to join in a discussion on the penal code, but he told them that the best thing for the government would be the Ten Commandments, especially those on stealing and adultery. He left the room and went to the village back home, and the boys from his childhood surrounded him and threw dirt at him, and he fell on them with a rock in his hand; but Adila grabbed his hand, saying: I am your wife, don't hit me; and he asked her about their daughter and she said: She's gone before us to Paradise, and walks among the immortals, giving them sweet water to drink, and that made him so happy; and he told her that a long life had ended, and he was trying in vain to remember that, and remember that the way to heaven was bordered with evergreens, and you could not walk along it at night, but a car could go the whole way in seconds which were ghastly with fear; and the person screamed but his voice was trapped in his throat and no one heard him and he flew through the air and landed on the branch of a tree; and he said: It was you! And she said: How did you not know? The night was so pitch-black, he said, I couldn't see a thing; and he talked a great deal to no avail; and she said: Tell me what you want, and he said: I want what I was looking for all over the houseboat—but here it is now coming in the shape of a dark cloud; there will be just one downpour, but it will be enough to slake the thirst of one roasting in torment; and then he stretched out his arm toward her, but he spotted Amm Abduh coming from the far end of the road, running as fast as he could, so he ran too, without stopping or turning around, but all the time he felt that the old man was about to catch him; and he reached the houseboat and rushed up the gangway and locked the door behind him, and found to his astonishment that everyone was there, the brothers laughing together as usual; and he embraced them, unable to believe it, and said to them: I had a terrible dream, and Ragab asked him what he dreamed; and he said: I dreamed that we were all in your car, and you were driving us along madly, and we hit a man and he flew through the air; and they laughed for a long time; and Mustafa said: Arrange the bedclothes properly the next time you go to sleep; and he sighed, and said: Let me smoke; and Samara offered him the water pipe, for she was looking after him now; and he took such a deep drag, it made his head spin, and he began to laugh at her and say: Did we not tell you? And she pushed the pipe away, and stood up and wound a scarf around her hips and began to perform an Egyptian dance; and he called on them to clap their hands, but found none of them there—indeed, there was no one else on the boat apart from the two of them, so he clapped for her on his own, and then he took her in his arms, saying: I've been looking for you everywhere, and I asked Amm Abduh about you; and at that moment there came blows pounding on the door, and Amm Abduh's voice was heard, shouting: Open up! And he dragged her by the hand to the refrigerator and they squeezed themselves into it, then he shut the door, and the pounding became more violent until the whole place began to quake, and the quaking went on until he opened his eyes and saw his colleague shaking him.

"Wake up!"

He rubbed his eyes.

"Go to the Director General," the colleague said. "He wants to see you."

He looked at his watch. It was nearly ten. He staggered to his feet, his heart sinking. He went to the washroom and washed his face, and then he went to the Director General's office, and presented himself to him. The man fixed him with a cold look. "Sweet dreams," he said.

Pain and self-disgust prevented Anis from speaking. "I saw you with my own eyes," the man continued, "as I was passing through your department. Sleeping like a baby."

"I am ill."

"You should have taken the day off."

"I did not feel ill until I got to work."

"The truth is that you are chronically ill. Incurable, in fact."

Anis was seized by a sudden anger. "No!" he shouted roughly.

"Are you addressing *me* in that tone?"

"I said that I am ill! Do not make fun of me!"

"You have gone insane—there's no doubt about that."

And Anis shouted, in a voice like thunder: "No!"

"You madman! This is where your addiction has got you!"

"It would be better if you held your tongue!" Anis retorted.

The man leaped to his feet, his face pale. "You insolent man!" he shouted. "You evildoer—you drug addict!"

Anis, without thinking, seized the blotter and threw it at the Director General. It hit him on the chest, on his tie. Shaking, the Director General pressed a bell.

"If you had said another word," shouted Anis, "I would have killed you!"

Back in his own office, he encountered a heavy silence. He met nobody's eyes. He sat down stony-faced, completely cut off. He did not even feel the pain.

Shortly before the end of the working day, a colleague approached him. He spoke to Anis in a sympathetic whisper. "I am sorry to inform you that there has been an order for your dismissal, and that you are to be sent to the civil service tribunal."

17

He surrendered himself to the fates. It was the worst calamities that made you laugh.

While he was eating his midday meal, Amm Abduh told him that he had not managed to buy anything from the dealer. They had erred in ignoring his warning. What to do? He would try his luck with another dealer, but he could not be sure of the outcome.

Disasters gathered like winter clouds. He lay down on his bed and skimmed through a few chapters of a book on the age of martyrs. He read for a long time, but sleep did not come. Martyr after martyr fell, but sleep eluded him. Lying there became detestable. He rose, and began to prepare the room for the evening, to pass the time.

When disasters rain down like this, one cancels out the other. A mad joy with a strange taste takes hold. You can laugh from the bottom of a heart which no longer knows fear. And, what is more, the pleasant diversion of the civil service tribunal awaits! What is your full name? Anis Zaki, son of Adam and Eve. Age? I was born a thousand million years after the earth. Job? Prometheus Drugged. Salary? The price of twenty-five kilos of Egyptian beef. A dealer must be found, at least.

He went out onto the balcony. Amm Abduh's voice

caught his ear; he was leading the afternoon prayer. He stood there like a mountain, dwarfing the rows of worshippers. There was a night watchman, a villager, a servant . . . A fleet of sailing boats, loaded with stones, was plying upriver. A wash of greenish-brown waves lapped monotonously, calmly against the houseboat, as if peace ruled the world. Acacia trees stood straight and tall along the bank like blessings, part of a different world.

Amm Abduh came in after the prayer, but found the room already prepared for the evening. Anis returned from the balcony. "You were chasing me, old man!" he said jokingly.

"What?"

"I dreamed that you were chasing me!"

"All's well with you, I hope?"

"What would you do if I sent you away from the boat?"

Amm Abduh laughed. "Everybody loves Amm Abduh," he said.

"Do you love the world, old man?"

"I love everything created by the Merciful."

"But sometimes it is hateful. Is that not so?"

"The world is beautiful, God grant you long life."

"Make sure you don't come back empty-handed."

"Our Lord is present."

The boat began its familiar shaking. Anis looked toward the door, to see who was coming early. Hardly had Amm Abduh left when Samara appeared. She looked harried and pale, her eyes full of apprehension and worry. The bloom of youth had dulled in her face. She shook his hand mechanically. Then they sat down, at some distance from each other. She noticed the room, prepared with extraordinary care for the evening. "Can life really go on as before?" she murmured.

"Nothing is as it was."

She closed her eyes. "I did not sleep for a minute."

"Neither did I."

She sighed, and then said: "Something irreplaceable has died in me."

"I have been hounded by death as well."

She held out the evening paper to him. "The body of a man in his fifties," she said. "Half naked. Sustaining fractures to the spine, legs, and skull. Hit by a car. The perpetrators fled. His identity, and therefore next of kin, have not been discovered."

He read the article, and then threw the newspaper aside. "We are back in hell again," he said.

"We never left hell," she replied.

"We never left hell," he echoed.

"We are really murderers."

"We are really murderers. And what is more," he continued, looking out at the Nile, "I am as good as jobless now." And he told the story of the Director General. They exchanged lifeless looks as she said how sorry she was.

"Have you any other source of income, apart from the Ministry?" she asked.

He laughed, in a way that dispensed with a reply. "Our friends pay the rent on the boat, and the expenses of our evening parties, but . . ."

"It is rare that someone is actually dismissed."

"He will tell every living person that I am a degenerate. A drug addict!"

"How dreadful! One catastrophe after another."

They withdrew into themselves.

And then the houseboat shook, again and again. The friends all came in together, and their faces were strange.

They fear trouble from Samara, Anis thought. Ragab asked him, pointing to the water pipe, why it was not filled and lit, and he replied that there was nothing to put in it. He thought: He's trying to make light of it, but in vain. It seemed that they all knew about the newspaper report, and it was not long before they also learned of his downfall at the hands of the Director General. "What disasters!" sighed Ali.

"We must get rid of the pipe immediately," said Ahmad earnestly.

They glared at him.

"The Director General could well organize a raid on the houseboat!" he argued; and then and there he rose to his feet, and hurled the pipe and the tobacco into the Nile. Then he threw himself down on a mattress. "We should consider this place a danger zone until things clear up," he said.

They looked at each other in undisguised misery. "Paradise has gone," said Anis.

And when no one replied, he spoke again. "That trip was doomed from the start. Why did you think of going out?"

"We must forget what is past," Ragab said sharply.

Samara snorted. "How can we forget, when there is a murdered man behind us!"

"That is why we must forget!" said Ragab harshly.

"It's beyond the bounds of possibility."

Ragab looked at her for a long time. No one knows what is going on in his head; no one knows about the trials of love. Could things get even worse than they already are? Ragab looked at everyone in turn. "I guessed what would happen here before I came," he said. "Now that we are at a distance from the event and at liberty to think calmly, we must declare our positions."

"I thought we had decided that it was all over!" said Ali in annoyance.

"It seems that Samara has another opinion!"

"Please don't go over all that again," said Saniya anxiously. "I'm completely broken down already."

"I spent a hellish night," added Layla. "We have a lot of suffering ahead of us. That is enough, surely."

Ragab said again: "But it seems, as I said, that Samara is of a different opinion."

Ali turned to Samara. The tone of his voice was grave and sad. "Samara," he said, "tell me what you think. We are all grief-stricken—agonized. None of us has had a wink of sleep. There is not one of us who likes murder, or could even imagine committing it. We share in your feelings, and the news has cut us to the quick. A poor man—perhaps migrating from the country. A stranger with no family. There is no way that we can right the wrong. How could there be? If it turns out that he has a family, then we will find a way of compensating them, but what can we do now?"

She did not utter a word; nor did she raise her eyes to his.

"Perhaps you are saying to yourself that our duty is clear," he continued. "Theoretically, that is true. We should have stopped, not fled; and when we were sure that he was dead, we should have gone to the nearest police station and made our statements of guilt, and then gone through the courts and paid the full price—is that not so?"

"Which in my case would be prison without doubt!" said Ragab.

"And appalling disgrace for everyone, including you!" added Ali.

"And even then the man would not rise from the dead, or benefit from our sacrifices in any way!" said Mustafa.

Ali spoke again. "I know you better than the others do," he went on. "You are an exemplary girl in every sense, but a little adaptability is essential if we are not to collapse under the burdens of life. This is an unfortunate accident, not a matter where country or principle is at stake. The question is simple. An unknown man was killed by mistake; and there is a responsibility which I do not deny. The stupidity of it is obvious. I wish to God it had not happened! But are we all of so little importance to you? Do you really wish to sacrifice our happiness and honor—and let me add, yours as well—for the sake of nothing?"

"I shall be good for nothing after this!" she murmured, sighing.

"That is a groundless fear. Thousands are killed every day without reason, and the world does not grind to a halt. You will always find opportunities for work, and a tolerant attitude toward us won't make you any less keen, or clever, or stop you from getting to the bottom of things—or anything else you care to name! Perhaps it will make you redouble your efforts."

"As do feelings of sin sometimes?" she said.

"But it is not your sin, at any rate; and these situations are apt to compel us to think about everything. Ragab has really developed, because of you, at least in his attitude toward women. Think on that. Be kind."

And she said, with great bitterness: "So I am going to certain death, then!"

"We are all going to our deaths," said Khalid.

"I mean a more appalling death."

"There is nothing more appalling than death."

"There is the death that seizes you when you are still alive."

"No, no! I will not allow us to be sacrificed because of a metaphor!" protested Khalid.

And at that point Ragab shouted in great agitation: "The newspapers will report that you were in the company of men with a bad reputation, out in the dead of night, involved in criminality, in murder! Doesn't that mean anything to you at all?"

His harshness enraged her, and she cried vehemently: "No, it does not!"

Now he became incensed. "This courage is a bluff! You know that we will all stand against you!"

"Lies!"

"Then off to the police station with us!" Ragab cried—and Mustafa bellowed furiously at him: "Everything we have just tried to do, would you, with your stupidity, destroy in one second?"

Saniya rose and went over to Ragab. She touched his hand to calm him down, and kissed his forehead. Then she stood in front of Samara. "Do you really mean to sacrifice yourself and us?" she asked calmly.

"Yes," Samara persisted, still angry.

"So be it," Saniya replied. "Do with us what you will."

But before Samara could say a word, Amm Abduh entered. Everyone was silent.

He gave Anis a small package. "I nearly wore myself out getting that," he said.

"Get rid of it at once," Ahmad told Anis.

"No."

"Well, I've had my say!" Ahmad said.

"There's nothing easier than throwing it into the water if we have to."

"What has happened?" asked Amm Abduh.

Anis gave it back to Amm Abduh for him to make a cup of coffee with it. The old man took it away. His arrival had subtly altered the atmosphere.

Silence reigned. Then Mustafa said sadly: "The evil eye is upon us."

"Let's roll a joint with it—who knows . . ."

Ali's face shone with a sudden optimism. "I bet that Ragab will have children!"

And then Anis laughed. He laughed in spite of his tense nerves. "You've made a mountain out of a mole-hill," he said.

And when no one paid him any attention, he continued: "Samara is a girl of principles, but she is also a woman with a heart."

They looked at him warningly, in open displeasure, but he continued to speak. "We are indebted to love."

More than one voice implored him to be quiet, but he concluded: "For it is love that has rescued us from the judgment of principles!"

Samara, irritated, muttered: "For heaven's sake!" and then burst into a storm of crying, as if her nerves had been suddenly ravaged. Ali approached her, moved by her distress, to calm her. As for Ragab, he had thrown himself at Anis, yelling: "You! You!"

And he gave him a great slap on the face.

18 ❧

Ahmad grasped Ragab's arm and pulled it violently back. "You're mad!" he said, his voice shaking. "What a calamity! What madness!"

Samara stopped crying. She gaped at them. There was a deathly silence. Anis took the slap without moving. He looked at Ragab for a long time without speaking. Mustafa started to approach him, to support him, but Anis put out a hand. "If you please," he said.

"It was a terrible thing to do," said Mustafa, "without the slightest doubt—but the culprit is a friend, he did not mean it. He was blinded by anger—"

"No!" Anis bellowed, with a voice like thunder.

Amm Abduh came, as if in answer to his call. "The coffee is on the stove," he said. Anis motioned for him to leave. Then he rose to his feet and began to pace back and forth across the room, and to speak inaudibly to himself. Then suddenly he leaped upon Ragab and fastened his hands around his throat. Ragab immediately struck at his arm to free his neck, but Anis butted him on the nose, and they lunged at each other, punching and kicking. The others rushed to separate them, but then Anis staggered and crashed to the ground. Amm Abduh appeared at the door, and stood looking at them, bewildered, muttering: "No! No!" Ahmad ordered him to leave, but he continued to repeat: "No! No!"—finally retreating under the pressure of their combined gazes, shaking his head miserably.

Mustafa and Ali helped Anis to an armchair. The others surrounded Ragab, who was wiping away the blood trickling from his nose. Anis placed his hands to either side of him, on the arms of the chair, and leaned his head against the back. He half closed his eyes. Layla and Saniya began to administer first aid. They fetched water and cotton to wipe the blood from Anis' lower lip and eyebrows, and they sponged his face and neck. As for Samara, her face was screwed up in pain, and she mumbled words that no one could hear. Ahmad struck one palm against the other. "I could never have imagined it!" he said.

"This is a catastrophe," muttered Ali.

"A demon has possessed us. Finished us off."

Saniya's eyes filled with tears. "Who would have believed this could happen on our houseboat!" she said.

Samara began to cry again, but without making a sound. Anis opened his eyes and stared sightlessly ahead. Ali bent over him. "How are you?" he asked, but Anis did not reply. "I will send for a doctor, if you wish," his friend continued, at which Anis replied: "There is no need for that."

"Misery has ruined us all, believe me," Ali went on. "Even Ragab himself. He would like to be reconciled with you."

Anis spoke, with a strange calm. "Nothing is important," he said, "except . . ." He swallowed, and continued: "Except the murder."

It seemed that none of them had understood what he

said. Anis sat up in the chair. "Are you feeling better now?" Ali asked him, and he replied with the same calm: "Nothing is of any consequence, except the murder."

"What do you mean?"

"I mean that justice must be done."

"But Ragab is fully prepared—" Ali began, but Anis interrupted him.

"I mean the murder of the unknown man," he said.

They looked at each other oddly. Ali shrugged. "The important thing is that you return to your old self again."

"Oh, I have, completely, thank you," Anis rejoined. "I am talking about what needs to be done next."

"But, my dear friend," protested Ali, "I don't understand what you mean."

"But what I am saying is not remotely ambiguous. I am talking about the unknown man, the one who was killed. I am saying that justice must be done."

Ali, confused, smiled idiotically. "You can see we are already as wretched as we could be," he said. "The only thing that could make it worse would be for us to be blown to bits."

"Justice must take its course."

"Speaking has tired you out, surely . . ."

"We must inform the authorities of our involvement at once—"

"You don't mean what you are saying!"

"On the contrary, I mean—and know—exactly what I am saying."

"This is incredible."

"You had better believe it, for it's the certain truth."

"But this has got nothing to do with you at all!"

"I am concerned by nothing else."

Ahmad brought Anis a glass of whiskey, which he refused with thanks. Ahmad then started to roll him a joint while the coffee was brewing, but Anis told him that he would do that himself when the time came.

"I beg you," Layla pleaded, "don't increase our misery!"

"There is no going back on it."

"But we had finished with all that—Samara herself had mercy on us!"

"I've said enough."

"Everyone," Khalid announced nervously. "We should leave. We've been touched by madness tonight. If we stay, something even more dreadful will happen!"

"But I will simply go to the police myself," said Anis. "Let that be known to you all."

They all stared at him, stunned. Ragab turned his face to the Nile to blow out his rage into the air. "You are not in your right mind," said Ahmad.

"I am, I assure you."

"Are you aware of the consequences of your actions?"

"Yes; that everyone will receive their just deserts."

"He's desperate!" Ragab bellowed at the top of his voice. "He's been fired! It doesn't matter to him if he brings the temple down on everyone in it!"

"Be quiet!" Ali shouted. "You are primarily responsible for everything, so don't say another word!" Then he turned to Anis. "Did you really imagine that we would abandon you in your trouble?" he said heatedly. "It's not yet certain that you have been fired. And if it turns out that you are, we're all behind you until you find another job."

"Thank you, but that's irrelevant," Anis replied.

"For God's sake, be sensible! There's not a reason in the world to justify your position! Even Samara has gone along with us! I don't understand you!"

"Do you really not understand?" shouted Ragab.

"Shut up!" Ali returned.

"Don't you understand that he is determined to take revenge on me!"

"Shut up!"

"He's gone mad—there's no use arguing with a madman!"

"We told you to shut up!"

"The heavens will fall on the earth and crush it before I permit an insane dope fiend to ruin my future!"

Samara opened her mouth to speak, but Ragab shook his fist at her angrily. "And what do you want to say, you root of all misfortune?" he shouted at her. She recoiled in terror, and then Ragab went mad. The bloodlust leaped from his eyes. "If there has to be an accusation of murder," he yelled, "then let there be a real murder!" At that point, all the men hedged themselves closely around him. "Disaster!" Ahmad cried. "There's going to be a disaster! We'll all be destroyed!"

Amm Abduh appeared again. "Well, praise the Lord!" he said.

"Get out of here!" Ahmad shouted. "Take yourself off, and make sure you don't come back!" When the old man had gone, he turned to Anis. "Anis," he said, "you can see what has happened. In the name of our friendship, declare that you do not mean what you say."

"I will never retract it!" Anis persisted.

"Well then, damn you to hell!" Ahmad shouted. He turned toward Samara, calling for her, with a look of terrified anxiety, to intervene. All eyes were upon her, clearly urging her to speak and also charging her with responsibility for what had happened.

She was overcome by grief and anguish. She looked at Anis, and swallowed. Just as she was about to speak, he said: "There's no going back, I swear that to you."

Ragab charged forward, trying to break the barrier they had formed around him, to fall upon Anis, but they stood all the firmer and grasped hold of his arms and waist. He tried with all his strength to free himself from their hands, but to no avail. And at that moment, Anis stood up and vanished behind the side door. He soon returned with a kitchen knife in his hand. He took up a position between the door and the refrigerator, crouched to defend himself to the death. The women screamed. Saniya threatened to call the police at the first hint of an attack. The knife redoubled Ragab's struggle, and he hurled insults and calumny on Anis. He tried again and again to attack him, until Khalid shouted: "We must leave at once!"

"I'll kill him before he kills me!" yelled Ragab. But they pushed him toward the door in spite of his resistance. More and more violently, he tried to free himself from them, and more and more doggedly did they prevent him, until there was almost a battle going on among them. He threatened to hit them if they did not leave him, and they in their turn threatened him likewise.

Anis watched the scene amazed. They were wrestling with each other. The beast wanted to kill. Desperately they tried to push him, and he could not overcome them.

Suddenly he desisted. He stood there, motionless, panting. Then he collapsed into a fury. Insanity gleamed in his eyes. "You think I alone am responsible!" he yelled.

"Leave the talking until we are off the boat."

"You fled with me!"

"We'll talk quietly outside."

"No, you bastards!" Ragab cried. "I am going myself! I will go to the police myself, and nothing will stand in my way—not ruin, death, or demons!"

And he rushed out, the other men at his heels. Saniya and Layla immediately followed them. The boat rocked and shook convulsively under heavy, angry feet.

Anis put the knife on the table and went over to the nearest mattress, where he sat down, not far from Samara. They both gazed out at the night, giving themselves up to solitary silence. They did not exchange a look or a word. The earth itself has quaked, he thought. Almost split apart. He became aware of the approach of familiar footsteps. He did not turn his head until the old man was standing behind him. "They have gone," he said.

Anis did not reply. Amm Abduh spoke again. "The devil had his fill of fun with you tonight." Anis did not break his silence. "I have brought the coffee," said Amm Abduh.

Anis fingered his jaw. "Leave it in front of me," he said.

"Drink it right away, from someone who wishes you well. It will soothe the pain." And Amm Abduh lifted the cup to Anis' mouth for him to sip. "Let it be for your good health this time," said Amm Abduh. Then he retreated, but at the door he paused. "I had made up my mind to break the moorings if he hit you again!" he said.

"But I would have drowned along with all the others!" Anis replied, astonished.

"At least there is protection in the Lord," said Amm Abduh as he left.

Anis laughed faintly. "Did you hear what the old man said?" he asked Samara.

"Do you not think we should call a doctor?" she asked in turn.

"No, no. No need for that."

Talking about it stirred up the pain again, but it was trifling now that the coffee had settled in his stomach.

"Will he really go to the police?" Samara asked.

"I have no idea what is happening outside," he replied.

She hesitated a little before saying: "What made you . . . ?" And then she stopped short. He had grasped her meaning, but he did not reply.

"Was it anger?" she asked.

"Perhaps."

"Perhaps?"

He smiled. "I also wanted to put it to the test—saying what should be said, that is."

She thought for a moment. "Why?" she asked.

"I don't know exactly. Perhaps to examine the effect."

"And how did you find it?"

"As you saw."

"Are you really going to inform the police if Ragab does not do it?"

"You don't want that!"

She sighed. "It all got beyond me. I was defeated."

"But the experience proved that it is possible?"

"But it appears that you will not follow it through to the end."

"I haven't the reasons that you have for that!"

"Now you're killing me all over again!"

He was silent for a while. Then he said: "You love him. Is that not so?"

She took refuge in silence and pretended to be unaware that he was waiting for her to speak.

"Have you found him different from the excellent man you refused before?" he said next.

"I see you still have your fighting spirit!" she said plaintively.

"There is nothing to be ashamed of, if you have found him different. He's still an excellent man . . ."

"But he has no morals!"

"They no longer exist. Not even for Ahmad Nasr."

"I'd like to call you a pessimist, but I have no right."

"At any rate, their amorality will protect them from committing any moral stupidity. And you will come to love again!"

"Torment me all you like; I deserve it, and more."

He laughed, and the laughter made him feel the pain

in his jaw. "I have a confession to make," he said, "which is that jealousy was one of the motives for my strange behavior!"

She stared at him in astonishment. He smiled, and continued: "It would not be right to deceive you. You might have imagined that one of the characters of your play had developed to its opposite extreme through the influence of your words—or by hard experience. And that would land you with a false ending."

She was still staring in amazement. "There is another ending," he continued, "no less trite than that—which is that you love me back."

She lowered her eyes. "And how do you see the ending?" she asked.

"That is our problem," he replied, "not simply a problem of the play."

"But you spoke earlier of 'saying what had to be said'!"

"That is true. It was not just anger; nor was it just jealousy. But I decided then to say what had to be said. To take a serious position in order to examine the effect. And there came an earthquake whose consequences none of us could have known. Even you were defeated!"

"You've killed me already—you're mangling my dead body now!"

"But I love you!"

A look of profound grief came into her eyes. "I confess," she began, "that I try to be more serious than I really am."

"Speak now—quickly. The coffee is about to take effect."

"In my moments of leisure, absurdity gnaws at me like a toothache."

"That's one of its symptoms."

"But I fight it with my intellect and my will."

"Perhaps you will find the development you need for your play in the moral collapse of the heroine!" he said ironically.

"On the contrary! No! I am determined to go on!" she protested.

He was silent in sympathy. "And even so," she continued, "I am convinced that the question is not simply one of intellect and will."

"What, then?"

"Do you know what it's like, the big wheel at a fairground?"

"No."

"It takes the passengers up from the bottom to the top, and down again from the top to the bottom . . ."

"And so?"

"When you are rising, you feel an automatic rising sensation, and when you are sinking, you feel an automatic sensation of sinking, in both cases without the intervention of intellect or will!"

"So give me an explanation for all this, and remember the coffee!"

"We are the people descending."

"And what can we do?"

"We have only will and intellect."

"And defeat as well?"

And she said, vehemently: "No!"

"Do you consider yourself a model of victory?" he asked her.

"Among those who are going down, there are some who surpass themselves—even who destroy themselves in the attempt."

She began to speak about hope. He looked out at the Nile. The night fluttered its wings, and its secrets were scattered like the stars. Her words died to a whisper echoing in the slumber of his dream. Before long, he knew, the dark waters would part to reveal the head of the whale.

She said to him: "You are no longer with me."

He said, and he was talking to himself: "The cleverness of the ape is the root of all misfortune. He learned how to walk on two legs, and his hands were free."

"That means that I should leave."

"And he came down from the apes' paradise in the trees to the forest floor ..."

"One last question before I go: Do you have a plan for the future, if things get difficult?"

"... And they said to him: Come back to the trees, or the beasts will get you."

"Do you have the right to a pension if—God forbid—you are actually dismissed?"

"... But he took a branch in one hand and a stone in the other and set off cautiously, looking away down a road that had no end ..."

About the Author

Naguib Mahfouz was born in Cairo in 1911 and began writing when he was seventeen. A student of philosophy and an avid reader, he has been influenced by many Western writers, including Flaubert, Balzac, Zola, Camus, Tolstoy, Dostoevsky, and, above all, Proust. He has more than thirty novels to his credit, ranging from his earliest historical romances to his most recent experimental novels. In 1988, Mr. Mahfouz was awarded the Nobel Prize for Literature. He lives in the Cairo suburb of Agouza with his wife and two daughters.